Mother of Wild Beasts

Mother of Wild Beasts

A Novel

E. Piotrowicz

RESOURCE *Publications* · Eugene, Oregon

MOTHER OF WILD BEASTS
A Novel

Resource Publications
An Imprint of Wipf and Stock Publishers
199 W. 8th Ave., Suite 3
Eugene, OR 97401

www.wipfandstock.com

PAPERBACK ISBN: 978-1-6667-0375-7
HARDCOVER ISBN: 978-1-6667-0376-4
EBOOK ISBN: 978-1-6667-0377-1

JULY 7, 2021

For my mother with love and gratitude

Contents

PART I

1 Doctor | 3

2 The Red Sofa | 8

3 Summer to the Rescue | 14

4 Cat the Dog and Crazy Magda | 19

5 Obsession | 26

6 Puddles and Pickles | 30

7 In the Garden | 36

8 Rain in the Desert | 48

9 Autumn | 56

10 The Birds | 63

11 The Weight of Love | 71

12 Christmas | 77

13 What Happened to Baby | 81

14 Mother of Wild Beasts | 88

15 The Dream | 94

16 Pandemic | 99

17 Cactus Dream | 106

18 On the Road | 109

PART II

1 Taken | 115

2 Maxim and Blaise | 119

3 The Unattended Moment | 125

4 Two Paths Converge | 128

5 Visitation | 145

6 The House | 151

7 The Desert Cave | 154

8 The Decision | 159

9 The Old Magnolia | 164

10 The First Visit | 167

11 Phyllis | 172

12 The Prodigal Son | 176

13 Bad News | 182

14 The Call | 186

15 Into the Desert | 190

Part I

1

Doctor

Summer wasn't easily perplexed. A naturally probing mind empowered by massive amounts of caffeine had ensured that every question mark in life would soon be a period and every task a check on her list. But that day in the nursing home, she had no answers, sitting across from Phyllis in the recreation room, that silent question on the faces, all of them looking at her expectantly. Why at her? She didn't know what was going on any more than anyone else. The letter hadn't cleared up anything. There were no words, no explanations, and no amount of research could have provided clarity.

Summer felt ill from the weeks of poor sleep and the questions that bullied her mind—a mind too weak and exhausted to contain, let alone answer them. She hadn't believed anything would happen, at least not to Magda. She had lost too much already. Surely she deserved to at least keep *her*. But when she took the call that fateful morning, with that ragged sunrise that looked like the end of the world, and her toothbrush still in her hand—when she saw the ambulance and its disconcerting lack of hurry . . . It wasn't right. It defied logic, reason . . . it defied science, which doesn't brook defiance easily. It defied justice. Nevertheless, there was Phyllis and the faces and the questions she couldn't answer.

All Summer knew with certainty was that things like this didn't happen in real life. If they did, they happened to someone else: someone far enough removed that the report could always be tucked away in that mental file marked "anomalies," seldom worried over or even reopened. Nevertheless, it *did* happen, and she was there, all the while thinking about other things—until she could think of nothing else.

***

"Tell me a little bit about yourself, Summer. What made you decide to go into mental healthcare?"

"I would say my direction suggested itself naturally early on. My parents both suffered from major depression, which went untreated for most of my childhood. But I studied psychology initially with the intention of working with children rather than grown-ups. I always saw myself helping children who were sad or confused, or angry. That's how I ended up moving to Atlanta for my MD, specializing in pediatric psychiatry. But some things have . . . developed—this past year in particular. I wrote about it in my letter. That's why I'm seriously considering this . . . well, this change in direction."

"It would be a change—a dramatic one. I wouldn't want you to enter into anything hastily, especially since you've spent a lot of time and energy—really your whole young adulthood—getting to where you are today. You've worked hard and acquired the academic credentials. You could work with children now, as you'd planned."

"Experience is often a better teacher than academic coursework, I'm sure you'd agree. It's the experience I noted in my letter that really brought me to this point. My earlier choices were more about careerism and getting a valuable clinical experience under my belt, until last year, that is. Not to say I didn't believe in the work and the good it could do, but I'm a different person than I was. I feel something now—something I've never felt before. Not a motivation to be impressive and professional and respected and affluent . . ."

"What is it that you're feeling now, would you say?"

"I'm not sure I have the words to explain it very well. I want to be small . . . no that's not it. I'm already small, but I want to be okay with that. I feel like if I can accept that I'm small, maybe I can have a chance at being whole. I want to learn and to heal."

"That's a good answer. You know this decision can't be taken lightly. You may be responsible for a great many small tasks beneath your dignity and education before you ever do anything you may be picturing in your mind. It's a life of unsung, unpublished knowledge. A depth of silence and service. Not a path on which to find greatness or glory by any means. For us, the way up is the way down, and many have failed to stay the course. It may do you good to come and stay a while before you decide. It may be that we are a good deal smaller than you think you'd like to be."

"The way I feel now, I doubt I would ever want anything else."

"Feelings aren't always trustworthy. But come. Stay with us a while. It was a pleasure talking with you, Doctor."

***

Doctor. Summer was still getting used to the title—its peculiar texture and flavor. Something about it made her dip her chin to hide a blush, almost ashamed. But why should she be? She had always thought she would wear it more naturally—she had worked so long and hard for it—but it was a title that felt as unreal as the letter admitting her into her undergraduate program eight years ago.

Her parents never went to college. They were a little skeptical of the whole institution when Summer came home from school one day with a folder filled with fliers and applications, repeating seemingly audacious advice from her guidance counselor. Summer had taken a test that said she was academically inclined, and there were scholarships and grants and work-study jobs for kids like her. Her father didn't see the point, and her mother cried a little. It was as though she was betraying them somehow, leaving home and the path they had taken. After all, wasn't that good enough for her, too?

Summer had been born in the summertime, and although she didn't remember the event herself, she always felt her name was a bit obvious and lacking in creativity. As the story went, she had been chubby and tended to fuss. She was afraid of the moon and the hissing Persian cat next door, but the moon she eventually came to accept. Cats, she would always suspect of nefarious intent. Her first memories were happy and mostly of food, though she never knew why until a recent psychotherapy session.

It was when she was twelve that Summer realized her family was poor. Children mostly don't notice these things until they start comparing themselves to their friends. Summer's friends had new clothes and toys, tall tidy houses, and cars that always started and never smelled bad. Their mothers stayed home and cooked hot meals from scratch, and their fathers wore suits and ties. Both of her parents worked multiple jobs, and she was their only child. She remembered asking for a little sister one Christmas, but her parents said those were far too expensive. She got pink socks and a Pez

Machine instead that year. She still had the Pez Machine in her home study, next to a bowl of expensive individually wrapped chocolates.

She had kept it, the worn smiling head of a famous mouse, initially as a reminder of what she had been and to motivate her never to slow down—to keep climbing. She had tasted success, and it tasted like expensive chocolates. She had developed an instant taste for it, and she kept the toy to remember everything she was leaving behind—everything that tasted like failure.

With her parents' reluctant blessing, Summer became the first in her family to go beyond high school. Ever since completing her undergraduate program and moving across the country, she had sent her parents baskets at Christmas, full of fancy foods they would never have had when she was a child. It had been a declaration of her new status—a signal of wealth, intellectual and cultural, and soon to be monetary as well.

Looking back on the past few years now, all of that seemed incredibly foolish. Summer groaned to think of what she'd said and done to assert her individuality from them—her superiority. Now she kept the Pez Machine as a painful reminder of her own pride and arrogance.

Growing up in the high desert city of Albuquerque with few chances to travel before she left home, Summer had always had a fascination with trees. Of course, there were trees in Albuquerque, particularly the cottonwood Bosque along the Rio Grande River, where Summer would walk as a girl, always pretending she was somewhere else. In her mind, she pictured herself as a grown-up woman, wearing clothes that were not only fashionable but brand new—not from the thrift store or handed down from a family friend. She pictured this well-dressed young woman walking in a forest full of deciduous trees, overgrown with ivy and moss, down a trail lined with giant, red speckled toadstools. A light, refreshing rain would begin to fall on her, and she wouldn't even care because rainfall was so rare in the desert, and she wanted to feel it on her face and let it soak into her bones.

Summer would walk in this magical fantasy wood, through the light veil of rain, to a little brick house with green trim and a shiny brass knocker on a polished green door where she would sit by a crackling fire with a steaming cup of peppermint tea. Her house was filled with nice, new, beautiful things, smelled like Thanksgiving all year round, and there was a tall, black Friesian horse in the backyard that she could ride whenever she wanted. And, of course, she had a purple sports car to drive to her amazing job as a chocolate taster at a fancy candy shop.

Aside from the opportunities afforded her there, Atlanta's reputation as a city in a forest had finally decided Summer's move those four years ago. In many ways, she had been living her childhood dream, down to the trees, ivy, and rain, and of course, now she could eat chocolate whenever she felt like it, though no one paid her to do it. She had rented a little brick home in a treelined neighborhood where she aspired to own someday. The day she unlocked that door and took residence there, Summer was tangibly moving up in the world, realizing her dreams and ambitions, ready to become a real professional helping all the sad little children. The year was 2019.

2

The Red Sofa

Descending through clouds that hovered like whipped cream on a steaming cup of hot cocoa, Summer had her first glimpse of the "city in a forest." From the air, it looked like a lot of moss-covered stones surrounded by puddles, and she thought it might be fun to get some rubber boots and go splash in them, but no—that would be childish. She hadn't been childish for many years now—or what felt like many years to someone only twenty-two years of age.

As the plane continued its descent, the mossy stones became hills, the puddles became lakes, and the moss itself became acres and acres of the trees she had longed for since childhood. It was finally happening, and it felt like a beautiful waking dream.

A shared ride deposited Summer and her luggage on the doorstep of a red brick house with green trim around the windows, green shutters, and a shiny green door with a polished brass knocker. It was truly incredible how perfectly it matched her childhood fantasy home, even down to the ivy crawling up the tree trunks. Retrieving the key from the pre-arranged location, she slid it into the lock and opened the door to her new home and new life.

***

"Can I help you with something, Miss?"

"Well, I'm looking for a sofa—a new one."

"All of our sofas are new, Miss. Did you have something specific in mind? What kind of space are you working with?"

"I'm renting a house. A lovely brick house near the university . . . it has a fireplace." Summer couldn't help mentioning the fireplace. She had looked forward to sitting by it on a couch that was definitely not a futon or previously owned.

"The university? Oh, well, we have some nice futons . . ."

"Oh, no. No, I'd like something more . . . sophisticated."

"Gotcha. Well, we have some nice leather sectionals, like this one here." Summer sank into one of the buttery showroom models, trying not to look shocked when she saw the price tag.

"Ah, yes, this is very nice . . . can I see some others? Or maybe I can just wander around a bit—discover them for myself?"

"I understand," and she really seemed to, which Summer found disconcerting. "You let me know if you have any questions, sweet girl." Oh no she didn't! Did that *girl* just call her *sweet girl*? It was either another one of those Southern quirks she didn't understand, or that girl knew! But how could she know? Summer had played it so cool! She was wearing her nice shoes! She couldn't possibly have guessed that Summer was on a budget and had never bought new furniture in her life! Her heart started beating faster, and her scalp was beginning to burn. No, now was not the time. She would have to chase it away. She breathed slowly, sat on the nearest sofa, and started to imagine a fire crackling in her new living room—a glass of whiskey, neat—and chocolate . . . with gooey hazelnut cream in the center. There, that was better. Summer opened her eyes.

"Looks like you found the one you like!" That girl was back. Summer hadn't even noticed what she was sitting on. "And that one's on sale!" Summer looked at it. It was comfortable enough. She could afford it. It was red, but she could work with that. Should she haggle? Was that a thing? She played it safe.

"I'll take it."

"Great! Now, this is very exciting—my manager says I can offer you two free throw pillows if you add on the maintenance plan."

"The what?"

"You know, if it rips or breaks or something, we'll fix it. Free of charge. It's worth having if you have kids or pets or might someday. And it's not a lot to pay." She handed Summer a glossy brochure explaining the plan. It did seem wise and forward-thinking. If something happened to her brand-new sofa, she could have it repaired for free! She didn't have kids or pets, but . . . no! That's ridiculous! Who gets a maintenance plan for a sofa? She was no greenhorn to be taken a ride and sold things she didn't need!

Summer felt a little sick when she swiped her debit card, but this was a big deal. It was her very first sofa, and it was new . . . and red.

***

The first attack is always memorable. For Summer, it was a day that would haunt her for years to come, every time she heard an ambulance siren—every time she went out for Mediterranean food. It was the day of her undergraduate graduation. Summer's parents took her out for dinner. She knew eating out was a luxury, so she tried to pick something cheap. They were just sitting there in the little Greek cafe—the one with the blue walls and the good spanakopita—just sitting there at the table eating and chatting about her future now that she'd finished her degree. There was a lull in the conversation. She took a sip of water and looked back up across the table at her mother when the lights flickered, but only Summer noticed.

It was as if her brain had experienced a brief power outage. She was gone, in a dream for just a second, and when she tried to tell her parents about what happened, her voice sounded distant and not like her own, like the sound of someone talking on the telephone. A wave of heat and dizziness came over her, and her head felt heavy and as though it were on fire. She stumbled outside and, feeling nauseated—hung her head down between her knees, and shut her eyes. It was like she wasn't even there.

She felt almost entirely cut off from the world around her. Her father had followed her outside and asked if he should call 9-1-1. She didn't remember saying it, but apparently, she answered yes because soon there was an ambulance there, and she was on it—only she wasn't. She was everywhere and nowhere all at once—anywhere except where her body actually was. She thought she was dying, and she cried.

All Summer could think about was what would happen to her parents if she died. Who would care for them when they were old? They wouldn't always be able to work, and she knew they couldn't have saved up much for retirement. They needed her, and she must survive for their sake.

The paramedics did an EKG and asked her questions. She saw the words she wanted to say, like text printed on her eyelids, but it was so hard to actually say them. They came out stuttered and slurred and slow when they came out at all. She got to the hospital and was shaking violently and crying when she actually realized where she was. They did a CT scan of her brain, blood tests, and a full stroke assessment. When the neurologist finally spoke to her, she said, "there's nothing wrong with you, but you seem to be having a severe panic attack. Do you experience a lot of anxiety?"

Summer felt incredulous. Sure, she'd had terrible anxiety for as long as she could remember, but it had never been like this. Still, she had studied psychology—she should have known what this was! They gave her IV fluids because the only thing physically wrong was that she was slightly dehydrated, then they sent her home. The episode lasted about 4 hours, but the bill would take four months to pay.

After that happened, Summer didn't want to venture out much at all. She didn't want to drive for fear that she might panic and cause an accident. She didn't want to leave her parents' house because she was afraid it would happen again in front of other people who would stare and wonder and possibly call another ambulance. She followed up with her doctor who prescribed her something for anxiety and something for depression and gave her some psychiatrists' names. It was soon after that when she decided. Medicine had helped her. Therapy had helped her. She wanted to be able to do that for someone else. Her B.S. in psychology wasn't enough. In a flash, she knew she had to go on to graduate school and become a psychiatrist.

***

It was Friday before the much-anticipated sofa arrived, wrapped in plastic, its legs in a bag with some screws. Summer had expected that it would come assembled and that the delivery men would just put it by her fireplace, and that would be that. On close inspection, she would need a power drill.

"Can I help you find something, Miss?"

"I'm looking for the power drills."

"Aisle nine. I'll take you." She could have taken herself, she wasn't a lost child, but she was too polite to refuse her guide. Summer examined all of her options and their prices under the employee's watchful eyes, trying desperately to look as though she actually knew what she was looking at. She picked up the second cheapest drill.

"Oh, you know, that one's not great, honestly. It's cheap, sure, but it's not the best design. This one works real well. It's the kind I use and it's lasted years." He picked up the second most expensive one and handed it to her. She pretended to examine it, nodding pensively.

"Ah, yes . . . thank you for your help. Well, please don't let me keep you from helping others. It could take me a few minutes to decide what I need."

"Okay. You just holler if you need anything, Hun." *Hun?* And he was definitely younger than her. It must be a Southern thing, but he really seemed to know. How could he tell? It wasn't as though she picked up the very cheapest one. She shouldn't have picked one up at all until he had gone. That was her mistake. Even though it wasn't the cheapest, he definitely knew. Her scalp started to tingle, and she had trouble focusing. She took a deep breath, massaged her temples with a little lavender oil from a tiny bottle in her purse, then she looked down the aisle in both directions, grabbed the cheapest power drill, and went to self-checkout.

***

After some trial and error, the couch was finally on its feet and cozied up by the fireplace. It looked a little smaller than she'd remembered, now that it was the only piece of furniture in the room. Still, she was pleased with its appearance. Being the warm, sticky June that it was, a real crackling fire seemed sadly absurd that evening. She tried playing a video loop of a crackling fire on her laptop computer, which she placed on the grate. It seemed like an adequate solution, but virtual fires turned out to be just as flat and dead and depressing as virtual friends. There was no warmth, no feeling, and no smell, so there was little comfort in it—only the magnification of an absence—a vacancy turned into a vacuum. Better to have no fire at all than this attractive unreality.

Finally, she settled on candles. Summer lined up three green forest-scented candles on the hearth and lit them. The flickering flames at least were real and living, albeit small. The little flames moved and glowed, making the room feel a bit less empty. Indeed, even a tiny flame is far better than a fake fire. At least she could whiff the smell of smoke when she blew them out. The pine scent wasn't very realistic, but the smoke made her eyes water when she extinguished them, reinforcing the flame's reality.

Summer poured herself a small glass of Irish whiskey, a drink that had always seemed upper-class and sophisticated in movies, unwrapped an expensive chocolate, and sat down on her new red sofa. She would need a coffee table next—someplace to prop up her slippered feet and set her empty whiskey tumbler or coffee mug. Maybe next month.

Summer gazed out the window into the blue-grey twilight and the leaves of her very own magnolia tree, now rustling in a gentle, tapping rain. She sighed. It was everything she had dreamed, this new life of hers, and yet Summer had never felt so lonely in all her life.

3

Summer to the Rescue

It couldn't be a cat; that much she knew. Summer never even entertained the idea, partly because of the hissing Persian cat she'd feared as a child, but also because of some unfortunate preconceived notions she never admitted to having, at least not out loud. Being a single woman living on her own, she decided her options for addressing loneliness did not include a feline companion because that would be, in her mind, a particularly miserable form of giving up. She did, however, want a companion—just not that kind. She had soon compiled a list of potential pets with pros and cons under each, gleaned through late nights of internet research. Her goal was to find an appropriate animal partner that could ease her loneliness without exposing her to unfair labels.

Summer quickly decided that a fish would be too much trouble for too little companionship, as she imagined herself scrubbing algae out of tanks and rinsing marbles in her kitchen strainer only to be scorned by a violently secretive betta fish. Her only pet as a child was a goldfish that swam in circles around a bowl full of pink pebbles. She had named it Florence, and it died after two months. She remembered not wanting to go into the hall bathroom for a few days after Florence's watery burial. Florence may have been short on personality, but the memory of her lifeless body floating in its bowl, then swirling down the toilet, still made her wince. No, fish were not for her.

Number one on Summer's shortlist of possible pets was a bearded dragon. Much of the appeal was in the name itself. Still, Summer also liked the idea of a prickly yet lovable reptile with a sarcastic yet faithful personality who might sit on her shoulder by the fireplace while she read and studied. Perhaps it could be named Eustace, Clarence, or Scrubb . . . maybe all three. Why couldn't a pet have three names—or was that sad and obsessive? She decided it was not obsessive but endearing and quirky. The mental image was most attractive as Summer cherished the idea of dispelling stereotypes and being considered by her peers to be a fascinating and complex individual. So, she took the obvious next step of visiting a pet store and meeting an actual bearded dragon. Having never met one personally, her knowledge of the species was limited to what contradictory information the internet could provide.

"Can I help you, Miss?"

"Yes! I'd like to meet a bearded dragon!"

"We don't have any dragons right now," the employee stated in a distressingly matter-of-fact tone.

"What . . . none at all?"

"Nope."

"Okay—what about chameleons?" Chameleons had been number two on the list. She liked how their eyes swiveled in different directions and thought their feet looked like little oven mitts. She would name hers Camille.

"We do have a chameleon, over here . . . there he is."

"He's tiny. Can I hold him?" The young man looked at her like she was insane . . . was that wrong?

"Well, he doesn't know you. Even when they're used to you, chameleons aren't really what you'd call friendly. Have you had one before?"

"No. How long before I could take it out and let it sit on my shoulder by the fireplace?

"Um, I have no idea. Chameleons like to be left alone, you know. Observed from a distance."

"But people do that . . . make their chameleons little string leashes and let them hang out on their shoulders. I've seen pictures online."

"Well then, it *must* be true," he said with a smirk. Summer decided she hated that pimply little snark. "But yeah. I've heard of people doing that when they raise them from babies." He looked her up and down and really seemed to see something. What did he see? "If you want something *snuggly*, you probably want a mammal, to be honest."

"But, full-grown or not, chameleons are cold-blooded," Summer protested. She wasn't giving up that easily. "Don't they want to sit on you . . . you know, because you're warm?"

"Look, I'm sure you've seen plenty online—pictures of dragons and chameleons watching TV with their owners, taking walks in cute little harnesses. Honestly, Miss, the only real stories I've heard myself are of chameleons getting loose and hiding in odd warm places, getting stressed out, and dying. The owners found them by the smell. Decomposing lizards are easier to find than live ones."

"Oh. Well, I can't have that. Essentially I want a companion animal that won't crawl away and die."

"Yeah, they aren't a beginner pet." She really hated the way he stressed the word *beginner* while looking her up and down.

A guinea pig, maybe?" Summer suggested. Guinea pigs were third on her list. She pictured carrying a jolly, chubby-faced rodent around in a pouch or a sling and taking it for walks around the neighborhood. She remembered a classmate having a pet guinea pig when she was in kindergarten. Its name was Twinkle, and she'd gotten to pet it once when it came for show-and-tell. She remembered Twinkle being soft but somewhat terrified of her. She imagined if it were her own, it would naturally adore receiving her affection. In her mind, she'd already named it Hamlet, Pig of Guinea.

"Well, you need a good amount of floor space for a permanent playpen. Piggies need specialized veterinary care—they are considered exotics, you know. They're fun . . . you'll probably need more than one, though. They tend to get lonely."

"Oh, but wouldn't I be enough to keep it company? I intend to play with it plenty."

"Oh, you're always at home?"

"Well, no, I won't be after this summer."

"But someone else will be home when you're gone?"

" . . . no."

"Then, no. They need more stimulation than you'll be able to give on your own. But if you want a creature that's okay by itself when you're out, will sit on your lap, and be fairly easy to care for, I highly recommend a cat." He looked her up and down again in that odd way that made her feel sized up and broadly categorized. She hated it.

"No, I don't want a cat."

"Allergic? Because there are hairless ones. Sphinx. They look a bit like aliens, but sweet, I hear."

"I'm not allergic; I just don't want one. It's not an option."

"Okay, not a cat person. Do you have a yard?"

"Yes . . ."

"Have you considered a dog, then?" She had considered a dog briefly but thought the idea seemed a bit basic and predictable. She wanted her pet to say something about her—that she, in fact, was neither basic nor predictable. She was a multi-dimensional and fully articulated Self—not some flat, thin, paper-person who did all the things the other flat, thin paper-people did . . . like owning a basic brown dog that did the usual basic brown dog things.

"I don't know . . . I don't think I want a dog. A bit boring, you know?"

"Boring? Naw, dogs are kind of the classic pet, you know—it would totally sit by the fire with you. Have you looked at the humane society listings?"

"The humane society? No."

"Well, you might want to take a look. There are lots of great dogs who just need a second chance, and the store will give you tons of coupons to get you started. We do training classes and grooming and everything you could possibly need. You really should think about it. Your friend might be waiting for you at the shelter."

Friend? Summer was a little offended by the thought that this pimply know-it-all thought she was looking for a friend. As though she didn't have any! She did—just not nearby. She very specifically wanted a pet, not a friend. However, at home that evening, sitting on her red sofa by her fireplace candles, something that the snarky kid had said kept coming back to her: There are lots of great animals who just need a second chance.

Now that was not so basic. In fact, it was very nearly compelling as she began to think of herself owning a three-legged-dog with a terrible scar or a missing eye. She could rescue a horrendously mistreated, abandoned, love-starved canine quite literally from the jaws of death and get a friend . . . or rather a pet at the same time. Her heart gave a little flutter with the refreshing altruism inherent in the notion of dog adoption and started scanning the humane society listings.

The night was turning into morning when she first saw Peanut's face and felt her heart start glowing. Peanut was an orphan who was picked up by Animal Control, wandering around a landfill, eating unspeakable rubbish, and smelling like death. There was something so tragic about her eyes. They were sad, pleading, lonely eyes, and Summer knew she had found someone as lonely as herself. Although just a puppy of four months, Summer thought the trauma of being abandoned for who knows how long at a landfill might have left her with some trust issues. She found that possibility all the more compelling considering the likelihood that she could heal this puppy's injured mind with plenty of consistent love and affection and mold her into a perfect companion.

One thing, however, was certain. That puppy was *not* a Peanut, but who was she? Laika, after the Russian space dog? Or maybe something Shakespearean, like Ophelia or Olivia? A thought came to Summer that seemed absurd at first, perhaps even a little dark. Surely it would be inappropriate . . . but then, why not? What was to keep her from naming her new puppy Catherine? Yes, Catherine was a beautiful name. Summer smiled faintly, feeling the threat of tears aching ever so slightly at the back of her throat. But why not? It wasn't morbid—it was just a name, and this would be a Catherine she could save. A Catherine she could hold and heal. Summer went to sleep that night, her heart still glowing with the anticipation of meeting her puppy the next day.

4

Cat the Dog and Crazy Magda

There was nothing average about the puppy peering at her from behind the chain-link gate. She was partially brindled like a tiger with one blue eye and one brown. A genetic mutation had caused her to sprout function-less dewclaws on her back legs, which looked a bit like rooster spurs. Peanut was a survivor—scrappy and intrepid—and she had a random look about her, like a collection of bits and pieces from vastly different dogs all patched together to create this impossible Frankenstein's monster of a puppy.

As soon as the four-month-old puppy squirmed up to her and licked her face, Summer knew this was the start of something glorious and good. She was saving a life—a weird, genetically mutated, and oddly-shaped life. This was the friend . . . or rather the pet for her. This was Catherine—but Catherine was a little too formal for everyday use. Summer smiled at the seed of an idea that had been steadily growing in her mind. As though this puppy was not strange enough, Summer decided to call her Cat. She liked the irony of it.

"Now remember, a tired puppy is a well-behaved puppy," the woman told her.

"I understand. Plenty of walks."

"Fetch would be better still, or playtimes with other dogs. She needs to run."

"Got it. Fetch and playtimes."

"That'll be good for socialization as well. She'll need plenty of that in the weeks to come. All kinds of dogs. All kinds of people."

"Socialization and exercise—got it."

"She eats half a cup of food three times a day right now, but that will increase as she grows, so keep track of her weight and adjust as needed. She's had her first three rounds of puppy shots, but you'll need to take her for rabies annually, lepto if you're letting her drink from the creek, and there is heartworm here, so treat for that monthly, along with flea and tick—a collar or topical is fine, but there's also a pill so just ask your vet about it. She just had her nails clipped, but you'll want to do that once a month, or have a groomer do it if you don't feel up to it."

"Let me write this down . . ."

"She's microchipped, but you need to transfer the contact info to your own—you can use the website in your folder."

"Microchip . . . vaccines . . . exercise . . . nails . . . feed three cups a day . . ."

"No, half a cup three times a day."

"Oh, right . . ."

"Just sign here, and you can be on your way!"

With visions of her happy fireside companion at the back of her mind, snuggled up warmly on her slippered feet, Summer signed the adoption papers, and with little fanfare, became a dog owner. Summer clipped a new purple collar around the puppy's neck and started walking toward the door. Naturally, Summer had assumed that the puppy would walk with her. After all, she was the one holding the other end of the new purple leash, but there was an unexpected tug when she reached the end. Cat was lying on her side, staring up at Summer with glazed, sorrowful eyes like a dead mackerel.

"Well, come on. Let's go." Summer gave the leash a gentle tug.

"Try getting down on your knees and calling to her."

"Come! Come on, puppy!"

"In a high squeaky voice. Sound excited. Dance around a bit." Summer looked at the woman skeptically. Was all of this really necessary?

"Come on . . . let's go . . . pup, pup, pup . . ." Cat lifted her head for a moment, then lay flat again. "You know, I think I'll carry her for now."

"Now, don't go spoiling her. She needs to learn how to walk on her own. She's going to be a big dog, you know."

"Well . . . wait, how big is she going to get?" Summer had assumed she would grow but hadn't thought she would be categorized as a "big dog."

"It's impossible to say with mixes like this. It's sort of a wait and see. I would guess medium to large . . . 50 . . . 60 pounds, maybe more. Is that going to be a problem?" Summer stared at the woman, then looked back at the one blue eye and one brown eye looking pitifully up at her.

"No, it's fine. We'll be fine." Summer scooped Cat up in her arms and carried her limp body outside.

***

A smiling puppy's face can radiate so many emotions: joy, contentment, mischief, love, and perhaps more than all the others, the mystery of its own potential. There is the sense that this comical creature still growing into its own baggy skin and over-sized feet somehow knows that it will grow up to be something noble, unique, even essential in its owner's life. But as Summer gazed into Cat's wrinkled face staring up at her in adoration, it was the puddle underneath her that she noticed.

"No, no! Bad Cat! No messes on the floor! That was bad!" Cat's introduction into Summer's life was chaotic from the start. Cat had christened the floor within five seconds of walking in and had discovered the wastebasket within five minutes. When Summer put her new puppy in the backyard to play, Cat quickly developed a fondness for digging and barking at squirrels, resulting in more scolding. "That was bad! No squirrels! No barking! And absolutely no digging! Bad girl!"

Summer remembered the shelter worker's words, which would become her mantra for the next eight months of her life: "A tired puppy is a well-behaved puppy." So, Summer took Cat to the neighborhood dog park to find some other puppies who might exhaust her and induce a long nap. She had seen a group of ladies talking while their dogs played most days and finally worked up the courage to take Cat. She entered the enclosure sheepishly, unsure of the proper protocol for introducing dogs.

"Oh, your puppy's so cute!" The dog park ladies squealed. "How old is she?"

"She's four months. She really needs some exercise . . ."

"Bring her in! What's her name?"

"This is Cat. I just got her." All of the dog park ladies laughed at the name, and Summer released Cat into the park. For a few minutes, Cat tore around the park's perimeter in circles, and Summer sighed. Finally, she would soon have a tired, well-behaved puppy to sit by her while she did some of her preparatory reading before her first semester of medical school.

"This is so good for the dogs. You should bring her every day to play. Everyone benefits—most of our dogs are still puppies (at least at heart) and need the run."

"I definitely will! Thank you!" Summer sat down on a bench and listened to the neighborhood gossip: domestic disputes, loud weekend parties, and stolen packages. As they sat and the puppies wrestled in the grass, Summer noticed an old woman walking purposefully up the street, clutching a sack-full of stones and acorns. Each time she approached the corner of the next house, she reached into her hoard and pelted the foundations. Then she calmly moved on to the next corner where she would repeat her ritual stoning. In this way, the old woman circled the neighborhood, mumbling to herself, and occasionally shaking her first at nothing.

"Who's that?" Summer asked.

"No, no—don't look! That's Crazy Magda!"

"Crazy Magda?"

"Shhh! Not so loud. Don't engage with her. Never engage if you don't have to. No, don't worry—she's not dangerous; she's just not all there. She does this every morning—just walks around the neighborhood throwing pebbles at all the houses, then she goes home. She doesn't do any damage, so don't worry about your house. Just don't engage. Don't look."

"Why shouldn't I engage with her?"

"No one does. She just says weird things. She may come by and offer to weed your lawn. Don't feel obligated; it's up to you. Most of us let her do it, and we give her a little money for her trouble. I'm sure she's glad of a bit of pocket change. She's always been here. I've been here fifteen years now, and she was here before me. She's just weird, that's all. Always has been. A bit of a loon. Probably senile." All of the women nodded in agreement. "Senile, most likely. But not dangerous."

"Maybe I should talk to her . . ." Summer mumbled, mostly to herself. "I am a psychologist after all . . . someday a psychiatrist. Maybe I could help her." Summer watched the old woman out of the corner of her eye, fascination growing in her mind, until Cat bounded up, tongue lolling.

"Look at your eyes! You're such a pretty girl!" As one of Summer's neighbors reached down to pet Cat, an instant change came over the puppy, starting like the low rumble of thunder deep in her throat. This was followed by the deepest, loudest, most terrifying werewolf snarl Summer had ever heard and an explosion of barking and snapping.

"Cat! No!" Summer grabbed Cat by the collar and pulled her away, which resulted in an angry scream and snarl as Cat tried to go back toward the woman and continue telling her off for trying to touch her. "Oh my gosh! I'm so sorry . . . I've never seen her do that!"

"Wow, no, it's okay. No harm done. You should really try to socialize her, though. Maybe get a trainer or do a class. That could become a problem if it's not addressed soon. I mean, she's small now, but . . ."

That evening, Summer checked out a tall stack of books from the public library about puppy-rearing, aggressive and defensive behaviors, and various training methods. She lit the pine forest candles in her fireplace. While Cat snored, stretched out on her side on the floor, Summer tried to figure out why her adorable, oddly shaped, genetically mutated puppy had turned into a dragon at the dog park.

***

Cat didn't like people. There didn't seem to be any rhyme or reason to it. Men, women, children, babies, tall, short, hefty, or slight—Cat would raise the hairs on her shoulders, all the way down to her tail and bark if anyone so much as looked at her. This came as a surprise to Summer since Cat hadn't shown any shyness, mistrust, or latent aggression during their first meeting at the shelter. Still, within a matter of days, Cat had decided that she wasn't a people person—or rather that she only liked Summer and hated everyone else. She had also decided that Summer's home, yard, and front sidewalk were her territory to protect from marauding squirrels, garbage collectors, mail carriers, and casual walkers who happened to pass while she was watching from the window.

Summer never expected to feel so embarrassed by her puppy. She knew she needed to get Cat out walking, running, and playing with other puppies. She knew she needed to socialize her, but she dreaded the moment when some well-meaning individual might say, "oh, what a cute puppy," and swoop in to pet her like they would with a normal puppy. This action would invariably result in vicious, deep-throated barking and snapping from the "cute puppy" and heart palpitations and mumbled apologies from her humiliated owner. After the first incident at the dog park, Summer had been too embarrassed to go back and had tried to get Cat enough exercise through long walks.

A conspiratorial thought crossed Summer's mind. Maybe the shelter had slipped Cat some kind of tranquilizer before they had met so that she would behave differently and have a better chance of being adopted—something to calm her and make her seem more normal. But Summer wouldn't let herself think crazy things like that for more than thirty seconds. Otherwise, it might spiral into an obsession, and she would end up spending hours of her life doing internet research. Of course, you can always find someone out there having the same crazy thought as you are but kooky enough to write an alarmist blog post or article about it. No, Cat had just bonded with her owner and decided to protect her from all other living beings on earth. There was something kind of heart-warming about that if Summer was thinking positively about it, rather than worrying and poring over books about canine behavior and training.

The problem remained that her puppy needed a lot of exercise, and without other puppies to play with, a lot of Summer's study time was taken up with getting Cat out to walk and chase balls in the yard. She felt she would have to be outside constantly, and her ankles were already covered in mosquito bites.

One late July evening, Summer sat in a camping chair on the back patio, watching Cat sniff around the back yard, jumping, snapping, trying to eat the occasional firefly that ventured near her. Summer chewed her lip nearly to bleeding, worrying about Cat's antisocial behavior until she heard a voice singing over the fence. She had been so distracted by Cat and her special needs that she hadn't realized she shared a fence with Crazy Magda. Indeed, she hadn't thought any further about the stone-pelting old woman since the day Cat first embarrassed her at the dog park.

The distraction was more than welcome. Creeping over to a crack in the wooden fence, Summer peeked through, trying to catch a glimpse of her neighbor. Through the crack, Summer saw a lush garden overgrown with prolific tomato plants, cucumbers, pumpkins, sunflowers, and a tidy stone path to a bench under an old apple tree, heavy-laden with young, green fruits. Magda was sitting on the bench in the twilight, singing softly. All around her, fireflies were gathering, blinking and glowing as if to her song's rhythm. The tidiness and beauty of Magda's garden seemed to belie the disorder of her behavior around the neighborhood. Summer wanted nothing more at that moment than to be sitting next to Crazy Magda on her bench with the fireflies and her soft humming, under the apple tree, without having to continually monitor her baby-dragon-dog. But that was a crazy thought in itself. It was just such a peaceful scene over there. So different from her own yard that evening. Summer wished she could be a part of it, somehow.

Reality interrupted Summer's momentary lapse as her mind began to explore the possibility of schizophrenia as an explanation for Magda's stone-throwing. Hallucinations. Delusions. And that was really what Summer ought to be concerned about anyway—Crazy Magda's mental health. What did she see, and why did she see it at every house on the street except her own? In her own garden, she simply sang and tended her plants surrounded by the glow of countless fireflies as though nothing in the world could disturb her peace. Strange.

5

Obsession

Maybe it was those four years of undergraduate psychology courses that made her want answers about why people did the things they did, or perhaps it was just a function of her naturally probing, caffein-powered mind. Whatever the reason, an obsession was born that night at the crack in the fence between her backyard and Crazy Magda's garden. From that day on, Summer became a keen observer of her neighbor's habits, from her pebble-throwing walk each morning to her odd jobs pulling weeds in neighboring yards.

Summer watched the old woman mumbling to herself as she worked at her weeding jobs along the street, hunched over the dandelions, pulling them up by the root and placing the weeds in a sack. She observed her plucking shiny green Japanese beetles off the crepe myrtles and rose bushes, plinking them into a painted pillbox she kept in her skirt pocket. Crazy Magda had more than pebbles in her pockets. Summer wondered what she did with all those beetles.

When evening came, Summer would crouch by the crack in her fence and listen to Magda singing under the apple tree with the fireflies, a picture of serenity. She couldn't pick out the words of Magda's song—they seemed to ramble on in a constant shimmering stream of color like the surface of a soap bubble floating on the breeze, self-contained, but without beginning or end, flowing in and out of itself. Summer would creep through the dark hallway in the dead of night to peer through her study window and see if Magda's lights were still on. Her house was never dark, although the curtain lace made it impossible to see inside. Did Crazy Magda ever sleep? Or was she afraid of the dark? It didn't have to be one or the other.

In her mind, Summer began assembling a case file on her neighbor. This mental case file soon turned into a collection of notes organized by type of behavior, conveniently color-coded in a binder. Her thought was that if she could collect enough data by observing Magda's natural, un-self-conscious behaviors—enough instances of repeated behaviors—she could assume data saturation. The saturation point would have to be a bit arbitrary, considering this ethnographic approach. Still, Summer was convinced that when data points (in this case behaviors) just went on repeating themselves, she could reasonably claim to have reached that point. Then, she could assume that any other observations would result in the same or similar data and use this data set to determine any trends that might help diagnose Magda. This all seemed well planned out, and Summer was feeling pleased with her research design until it became evident that an interview would be necessary to properly diagnose her.

That could be tricky. How could Summer get some face-to-face time with Magda to test out her theories? She needed to assess certain things that simply couldn't be observed but must be reported verbally. Should she go to Magda's door, introduce herself as a concerned neighbor, and see if she could ask her some questions? Summer may not have known a lot about how neighbors normally interacted, but she was reasonably confident that this approach would prove inappropriate. She continued to brainstorm different options for getting Magda to talk to her until a plan started taking shape.

Summer knew Crazy Magda's schedule and thought that if she were to take Cat out walking during "pebble-time," she might be able to find an excuse to interact with her. She could go counter to Magda's direction to not seem like she was following the old woman and thus meet her head-on. Summer thought this plan was the simplest and most straightforward, making it, therefore, the best. She would do it!

The next day, Summer clipped on Cat's leash and stepped out into the warm, humid morning. It had rained the night before, and there were earthworms on the sidewalks. Cat found them especially scrumptious and haphazardly jerked Summer from one worm to the next, peeling them from the pavement and slurping them down, despite Summer's disgusted protests. "Leave it, Cat! Yucky!" Summer had intended to seem so casual on that walk, but Cat hadn't run that morning and was bursting with energy as she wheezed and strained against her collar, torn between the temptation to tree squirrels and to feast on flattened earthworms.

"No! No pulling! Bad girl!" Summer hissed at Cat, trying not to make a scene as she approached Crazy Magda coming up the sidewalk. Cat had stopped to inspect a dead cicada. Summer tried to pull her away from it, but Cat planted her feet and slipped backward out of her purple collar. Leaping in the air with excitement over her freedom, Cat tore down the sidewalk toward Magda. Summer's heart raced as she rushed after Cat. She braced herself mentally for the confrontation that was bound to occur, as it always did when Cat met other people: the blood-curdling roars and barks and bared dragon fangs. This casual meeting couldn't be going worse. Soon Cat would be snarling and snapping at a potentially mentally unstable woman whose reaction could be anything from terror to rage!

"Cat! Stop! Come here! Catherine! You stop right now!" The puppy never looked back at Summer as she galumphed down the sidewalk and planted her front feet squarely on Magda's stomach with a little whistling whine issuing from the back of her throat. She wasn't barking yet, at least, but Summer expected some sort of outburst from the old woman—a scolding—maybe even a beating. She ran to catch up before the situation could turn any uglier. As she approached, she couldn't conceal her amazement. Cat was sitting politely in front of Magda, who had crouched down, speaking softly to her and stroking her ears. Crazy Magda looked up at Summer with a warm, jack' o' lantern smile of missing and discolored teeth.

"I stopped your dog."

"I see that—thank you very much! I'm so sorry—she got away from me."

"Yes, I saw. I told her she shouldn't run away from her Mama. She could be hurt by a car or frighten a child."

"That was bad, Cat!" Summer said, shaking a finger at the puppy.

"No, no, she's not bad—she's just a baby . . . a child herself. She's still learning what you want and how to give it to you."

"Well, thank you for catching her. She usually barks at other people. I'm surprised. She actually seems to like you." Magda smiled again and kissed the top of Cat's head.

"Thank you for coming to see Old Magda, Catherine. Next time you come to me on your leash with Mama. It's safer."

At that point, with Cat's collar back on and duly tightened to prevent another escape, and Magda rising again slowly to her feet, Summer remembered the reason for her walk. Now it seemed out of place to question her about the pebbles, but not wishing to waste the moment, Summer extended her hand.

"I'm Summer, by the way. I live in the house next door to you."

"Yes, I know. My name is Magda. I've lived in this neighborhood for fifty years! Can you believe it?"

"Oh my! That's a long time. I suppose it's changed a lot in that amount of time."

"No, not so much. The trees have grown. People come and go, and they look different—dress different—they are different, I suppose but all the same in many ways."

"Oh? In what ways?"

"Mostly what they bring with them. Catherine, don't pull Mama's arm. She wants to take you home now. Poor Catherine. She worries about you very much, you know."

"She worries about *me*? I worry about *her* constantly. This barking at other people is out of control."

"Well, you both worry. It's something you'll have to work out between you." Magda started walking away, reaching into her pocket for a handful of pebbles.

"It was nice to meet you, Magda," Summer called after her. The old woman waved a deformed, arthritic hand and walked on. Summer watched her pelt the foundations of the next house with the pebbles. Well, it was a start, at least.

6

Puddles and Pickles

It is difficult to describe to anyone who has not grown up in the desert the excitement Summer felt buying her first pair of rain boots. They were tall, red, rubber boots, and she bought an enormous red umbrella to match—not the kind that folds up and fits in a handbag, but a long, straight one with a broad canopy and a curved wooden handle like the kind in old movies where people danced and sang and splashed in puddles.

Since bringing Cat into her life, it had become clear that Summer would have to go out for walks no matter what the weather was doing—soupy heat or tropical storm. She had made the mistake of wearing her nice leather flats on a walk that had turned unexpectedly rainy and gave herself a neck spasm from clenching her teeth, worrying over whether the shoes would be ruined. They were real leather, and she had spent more money on them than she had ever spent on a pair of shoes, a fact which made her feel ill when Cat pulled her into a puddle that went up to her ankle. They were not ruined, miraculously. They took a day to dry, but her neck took three days of heating and stretching to feel normal again.

Summer had met Magda only once since their first encounter on the sidewalk. Summer had been sitting on her front porch reading a textbook on pharmacopsychotherapy when Magda strolled by on her way home after a morning of weeding. She carried a burlap sack full of dandelions and waved to Summer from her front gate.

"Good morning, Summer!"

"Hello, Magda! What have you got there?"

"Salad! Do you want some?" Summer was taken aback but played it cool.

"No, thank you. I'm just doing some reading right now."

"Yes, I see . . ." Magda said with a sly smile. "A good book, is it?"

"Very interesting."

"Are there animals in it?"

"Animals? No, it's not that kind of book. It's actually a textbook. I'm starting medical school next week. I'm going to be a doctor—a psychiatrist," Summer said impressively.

"I bet you like ponies best."

"I . . . there aren't any animals in it . . ."

Magda chuckled softly and waved again before disappearing behind her garden gate, leaving Summer blushing behind her book. *Ponies!* How old did Magda think she was, anyway!

***

Summer decided to wear her interview suit that morning. It was her nicest (and most expensive) outfit, aside from the bridesmaid's dress she had worn the year before in her college roommate's wedding, but a teal strapless ball gown definitely wouldn't send the right message on her first day of medical school. Summer wanted to be taken seriously. She wanted to look like she was already a professional—a professional in a long line of professionals. She wanted to look like she had grown up among the lettered folk, going to conferences where one of her parents might have been keynote speaker, eating truffled anything in restaurants with cloth napkins. She wanted to look like she deserved to be there—like her grandfather was on the board—like she'd scored a 528 on the MCAT—like she had known her life's direction since she was five. Summer had gotten up early and deliberated long over how she wanted to look on her first day. First impressions were serious business, and she wanted to give the impression of maturity, professionalism, intelligence . . . not like a little girl who loves ponies.

Why had Magda's silly words hurt her feelings? It didn't mean anything. Magda was always saying strange, inscrutable things out of the blue—it was why the neighbors avoided talking to her. Still, it kept coming back to Summer's mind as she stood in front of the bathroom mirror, agonizing over hair and makeup decisions. *I am smart. I went to college. I graduated at the top of my class. I am not a child. I am a grown-up woman achieving my goals. I deserve to be here. I am not a child. In four years, I'll be a doctor. Doctor Summer. I am not a child.*

Despite all the ways in which Summer explained away Magda's question (from dementia to some sort of personality disorder), Summer had avoided her neighbor for the past week. She still observed her and still took notes—still speculated and compared her observations with what she had read. But when the first day of medical school came, she couldn't stop thinking about Magda. She couldn't get those laughing eyes and stained, sparse teeth out of her head. *Ponies!* But Magda was disordered. Of course she was. Maybe Summer could help her when she figured out what the problem was. In the meantime, this was her moment! Her chance! Her first day of post-graduate study! She had arrived!

Still, whether Magda had meant to or not, she had found that little tender spot that Summer preferred to keep tucked away out of sight. That fragile pride in her accomplishments and how intelligent and mature she had become through her own hard work despite her background and socioeconomic challenges. She had made Summer feel like a little girl who thought she was so grown up and dreamed of taming wild ponies and making them gentle. And what was wrong with that, anyway? Summer wanted to help people. She wanted to help children who were hurting. That was real. That was honorable and absolutely respectable. And yet, as she stood in front of the mirror, adjusting her hair for the dozenth time, all she could see was a little girl pretending to be grown-up. She might as well wear pigtails—it was how she felt that morning.

But Academia is full of well-meaning individuals who specialize in stoking fragile young egos, for better or worse. That morning her advisor told her with great importance: "You are no longer a student, Summer. You are a scholar. You would not be in this program unless you were truly worthy." That was all it took to restore Summer's confidence, and her first day went by like a dream—a perfectly glorious dream where she always had smart things to say and correct answers to give. A dream where she really seemed to be the person she aspired to be, where classmates and professors were all colleagues, and her opinions were all respected. But as Summer unlocked the door that evening and stepped into her home, Cat rushing and wriggling up to her as if she had come back from the dead, the beautiful dream took a turn, plunging into the realm of nightmares.

"Cat! What did you do!" Summer spanked Cat's thigh with a loud smack. Cat put back her ears and tucked her tail. "That was bad! I'm so . . .

so . . . Cat! You bad dog! Bad! Bad girl!" She reached down to grab Cat's collar, but the puppy sprang away, tearing around the room in circles, dodging Summer's grasp. Summer chased Cat around the house, around the new coffee table, around the red sofa, until she finally caught her, shut her in the bathroom, and tried to breathe deeply from her lavender oil vial. When her heart stopped hammering, Summer assessed the damage.

Maybe if she had grown up with nice new things, it wouldn't have hurt so much. But Summer's heart sank, and the threat of tears ached in her throat as she examined the chewed-up arm of her new sofa, the mangled red rain boot that would never keep the rain out again, and the large wet spot on the carpet. There might have been other damages, but the sofa and boot were the most soul-crushing. She was a *scholar!* A young professional! She *deserved* to be in medical school, and what's more, she deserved a few nice new things in her life. She'd worked hard for them! Earned them!

Summer lay down on her bed, ignoring the pitiful whistling whines issuing from the bathroom. Maybe she should have gotten the maintenance plan for the sofa after all. There would be no free repair now. Maybe she should never have gotten a puppy to begin with. She didn't know it would be like this. Maybe she should just take Cat back to the shelter. Someone else could save her. Someone else could teach her to be good and make her into a friend—someone who knew what they were doing, had multiple pairs of nice new rain boots and money to spare for a new couch after Cat was done teething.

Summer thought up multiple versions of what she would say when she took Cat to the shelter and surrendered her: *I wasn't ready for the commitment. Our individual needs aren't meshing well. I don't have time to train her properly. My lifestyle isn't the best right now for keeping a puppy happy. I found out I'm allergic to dogs. I can't afford to give her the kind of life she deserves . . .* She continued brainstorming different excuses for taking her puppy back to the shelter until she heard a light tap on the front door. With a feeble sigh, Summer rolled off her bed and dragged herself to answer the summons.

Summer opened her door to find an empty porch. She looked around in both directions but saw no one and heard nothing but cicadas and a mockingbird singing together in the heavy evening air. Children's pranks weren't what she needed at all that evening. But as she started closing the door, Summer noticed a jar sitting by her welcome mat. She picked it up and examined its contents. The word *Pickles* was scrawled across the flat top. It must be from Magda. Surely none of her other neighbors could be responsible.

Random as it was, Summer realized that pickles were precisely what she wanted right then. She sat down on the stoop, still in her expensive interview suit, popped open the jar and ate its entire, briny contents, including the sprig of dill at the bottom. Thus fortified, Summer marched over to her neighbor's door, empty jar in hand, and knocked with confidence. Magda's head, wearing its customary dark green beanie cap, despite the heat, peaked over the garden fence, fuzzy gray braids falling over her shoulders.

"Magda," Summer exclaimed, handing the empty jar over the fence, "thank you for the pickles! I loved them . . . so much that I ate them all in one sitting. It's just been that kind of a day."

"I'm so glad you liked them. I thought they might help."

" . . . help?"

"You've had a hard day."

"Well, yes. Yes, that's very true. It was a good start to the school year. Better than I could have hoped, really. But Cat . . ."

"She missed you."

"You could say that. I don't think I'll be able to keep her after all. I like her. She has the potential to be a good companion, but she's been so much trouble! She chewed my boots and sofa today while I was gone!"

"She missed you."

"She left a huge puddle on the carpet. I think she might have been on my bed. There are hairs, and my pillows smell like her."

"She missed you very much."

"I'm going to be gone. It's just life. She can't be missing me so destructively. I'll have to return her. Someone else will take her, I'm sure." Summer said the words but doubted their truth, knowing Cat's attachment to her and distrust of all other humans, except Magda.

"I'll take her."

"What?"

"I'll take her for you when you're gone. She can be in the garden with me. Don't take her back. You know what happens to dogs like her—dogs who are damaged and only trust one or two people in the world. You need each other. Bring her to me—at least until she's grown and calmed down a little. Don't take her back."

"She's a lot of trouble, Magda—and strong. She could overpower you."

"I know my way around the wild ones. Bring her to me."

"What if she digs up your garden? I couldn't . . ."

"She won't. Bring her to me. Anytime. Just don't take her back to the shelter. She's a good girl, and you're good for each other. Trust me."

7

In the Garden

As the months passed, Summer continued medical school taking comfort in knowing that her belongings were safe from Cat's busy jaws. The problem of property damage being therefore solved, Summer grew to love the awkward puppy and shook her head with disbelief when she remembered how close she had come to surrendering her. Meanwhile, Cat grew. Her clumsy puppy paws started to fit the rest of her physique, and there came to be a noble, patient quality about her face. When Summer would return home at the end of her day, Cat was usually found lying at the foot of the apple tree in Magda's garden while the old woman tended her vegetable beds and sang the song she always sang—the song like a soap bubble, without beginning or end.

Cat showed quiet respect for Magda's garden, never digging up the soil or chewing anything except what was offered to her. When Summer released her back into her own backyard, however, Cat was seized with the desire to tear around the perimeter in circles before digging up unidentifiable delicacies from the dirt or attempting to devour the giant green snake that watered the flowers. Summer would scold her, of course, but the dog would turn to her, head hung low and eyes so injured and remorseful that Summer couldn't resist throwing her arms around Cat's neck and hugging her.

"She needs to know the rules, Summer. There have to be appropriate consequences, or she'll keep doing it," Magda would tell her.

"I tell her not to."

"And then you apologize for it."

"No I don't! She just looks so sad and chastened! I have to comfort her so she knows I still love her."

"She looks sad because she knows she did something wrong. Let her feel her mistake. If you coddle her, she'll think it doesn't matter. She'll stop caring about disappointing you."

"She's not that smart," Summer would say. Magda would just look down at Cat, shaking her green beanie cap and gray braids with a sigh.

While their interactions centered around Cat, leaving her and picking her up, Summer was not pacified in her professional interest. In fact, those who knew her growing up would have confirmed that Summer never let things go and could be a tad bit obsessive. Summer preferred the word persistent. It sounded less pathological. After all, where would she be now without that inner urge to chase down answers, to keep trying to better herself and her opportunities, and refuse to take no for an answer? Would she have gone to college? Would she have graduated summa cum laude or gotten into medical school? No, while obsession ranked as a potentially disordered behavior, even a vice, to Summer, persistence was the corresponding virtue she claimed. It was this very persistence that would help her crack the case of Magda's diagnosis. And now that she interacted with her a little most days, she had more natural opportunities to observe.

Summer continued adding to her notebook of behavioral observations, still recording Magda's routine, now adding quotations—things Magda said that seemed potentially meaningful. In this way, Summer collected consistent data and eventually felt confident that she'd reached saturation. She attempted a few levels of data coding but wasn't sure she was doing it right. After all, her classes had focused more on quantitative than qualitative research, and everything she knew about grounded theory or ethnography at that point had been self-taught. She needed a course in it. She'd bring it up with her advisor soon.

At least she felt confident in generalizing a few observations: that Magda did indeed pelt the foundations of every house in the neighborhood other than her own every day at the same hour, rain or shine, that she attended to her little gardening jobs with likewise regularity, sang in her garden under the apple tree at the same time every evening, and never seemed to turn off her lights at night. Summer tested the last observation for several nights by waking up every hour on the hour to check, peering through the blinds in her study. The house was never dark. She had a list of explanations, including everything from nyctophobia to general anxiety.

Considering Magda's age, of course, which was at this point merely a guess on Summer's part, it seemed possible that she was experiencing dementia. This could explain any number of Magda's inappropriate behaviors while leaving room for anxiety and even hallucinations, which would be exciting . . . at least as a case study. Perhaps she could write it up for a journal or something. It was just so hard to say anything with certainty without some sort of past baseline that might point to changes in her behavior over time. In other words, was this strange behavior worsening over time? When did it begin? The neighbor she'd spoken with briefly at the dog park—the one who had lived in the neighborhood for fifteen years—made it seem like Magda had always been this way. Since the neighbors all largely ignored her, they wouldn't likely notice little changes in behavior. Yes, perhaps dementia was the most reasonable explanation. Of course, Summer really needed to sit Magda down and talk to her before forming any conclusions.

Although Magda watched Cat regularly, it had never seemed right to ask for more of her time just to talk. She had her odd jobs—mostly pulling dandelions—and Summer hadn't wanted to interfere with her schedule, which she could tell was carefully and consistently followed. However, eventually, the time seemed right to seek out a real conversation without seeming suspiciously curious. They had interacted long enough; it shouldn't come as a shock that Summer would engage her in more personal conversation.

During Magda's regularly scheduled neighborhood weeding time one Saturday morning, Summer took Cat out for a little walk. She made it look natural, of course. She didn't just make a beeline for Magda but circled the block before stopping by the yard where the old woman knelt, pulling up dandelions, putting them all, as usual, gently into a little burlap sack.

"Hi Magda, how are you?" Magda ignored her. Interesting. "How are you this beautiful Saturday?" Still, Magda kept silently working and never looked up. Perhaps she was hard of hearing, though Summer hadn't noticed any signs of it before. Even so, she spoke a little louder. "Is everything okay?" Finally, Magda looked at her with a somewhat stern expression, as though Summer were a child who kept pestering her for a cookie too close to dinner time.

"I know you want to talk, but I need to be faithful to the job I'm doing right now. Come over this evening. We can talk then. Bring Cat."

"Okay, thanks, I will . . . sorry I interrupted." This was a better outcome than Summer had hoped. She felt a little scolded and childish, but she didn't have to fish for an invitation at all. Magda just invited her over—to talk! Summer was thrilled by the prospect of gaining a richer glimpse of Magda's inner life, making her diagnosis that much more confident. Summer walked Cat around the block one more time, just to make it seem on purpose that she was out and went back home to watch Magda from her front window.

That was one thing Summer had noted about Magda: she was single-minded and intense whatever she was doing. She never seemed distracted, never seemed to do anything half-heartedly, never seemed to be thinking of anything but the task before her. Granted, her tasks were not complex, so cognitive functioning was difficult to judge. With her absolute and unvarying routine and faithfulness to any odd jobs, her memory and ability to plan and organize her time seemed relatively healthy from what could be observed.

Summer went over her notes that evening, trying to decide how to question Magda without seeming like she had ulterior motives or suspicions. She needed some reason for wanting to talk with her, other than asking her questions about herself that could seem suspiciously personal. Her plan was perfect.

Summer went to Magda's front door that evening with a box of cookies. She knocked, waited, and knocked again. Finally, Magda's green beanie appeared at the side gate into her garden.

"Come back to the garden. Cat can play while we talk." Summer stepped through the gate into Magda's soul, or so it seemed. Usually, Summer had been tired and on a mission to collect her puppy, barely noticing the garden itself. This evening she really looked and saw that it was not a space kept by an agitated or disordered psyche. Everything was immaculately kept, from the stone pathway that meandered like a riverbed, branching through the garden and leading finally to Magda's bench under the apple tree, to the raised vegetable beds, like perfect little islands, dense with foliage and forming fruits. Cat trotted around the perimeter fence, more at ease and familiar with the space than Summer, nose to the ground, chasing the occasional squirrel.

"You're not from here originally. I can tell by your accent," Magda said, motioning for Summer to sit on the bench. "Where do you come from?"

"I moved here from New Mexico. Albuquerque. I grew up in the high desert."

"The desert!" Magda gasped.

"Yeah, as a little girl, I dreamed of leaving—living in a place like this, with rain and trees, and all that ivy and moss on everything. Frankly, I don't ever want to go back." Magda looked at Summer's face searchingly. She seemed to be on the verge of saying something but changed her mind. Summer finally filled the pause. "Have you always lived in Georgia?"

"Yes, I've always lived here, but I've spent many years in the desert, too . . ." There was that searching look again. "It was different for me, though. I didn't grow up there."

"Oh? What took you there?" Magda paused and looked deeply into Summer's eyes—more deeply than was comfortable and with a pause of unnatural duration.

"Exile," she finally said quietly.

" . . . exile?" Now, this was intriguing. The possibility of some sort of detailed delusion was making Magda's case more compelling by the minute.

"You brought cookies!" Magda noticed the box on Summer's lap and cracked a childish grin.

"Yes, should we open them? I thought you might like some."

"Beautiful! Now, what was it you wanted to talk to me about earlier? I could tell there was something you wanted to say."

"Oh, only that I hoped watching Cat wasn't taking away too much from your time. I'd like to compensate you. I've taken advantage of your kindness too long."

"Chocolate chip! Oh, these look tasty!"

"I'm glad you like them! Well, you are the only other person I know of who Cat doesn't absolutely hate. I don't know what I would have done without you these past few weeks. I don't know what I was thinking, honestly . . . getting a puppy right before starting med school! I'm really very grateful to you. She's been getting into far less mischief in the house, and I know it's because she's happier . . . cared for when I'm gone. I'd really like to pay you for what you do." Magda's eyes crinkled as she thought for a moment.

"Whatever you think is appropriate. I like Cat. It's nice to have her around."

"I notice you walk around the neighborhood every morning. Do you take Cat with you when you have her?" Summer asked innocently.

"Oh, no. No, Cat doesn't come for that walk. I'm working then, you know, and need to give it my full attention."

"Oh, I see." An interesting twist, Summer thought. Magda considered her rock-throwing to be a job she had to do—some kind of compulsive behavior, or better yet, a referential delusion, perhaps. "Who hired you to do that? Are you paid well for it?" Summer asked. Magda chuckled.

"No, no. It's not that kind of job. More of a responsibility. I do what I can."

"What is it that you're doing, exactly?" Summer asked, trying to sound casual. Magda looked at her with a cunning smile.

"Well, if you have to ask, then you don't need to know."

They sat silently for a little while. Summer tried to reformulate her questions to make them as natural as possible. In the meantime, the light began to fade, and evening started to close in on the garden. It was time, according to Summer's observations, and sure enough, Magda began to sing. It was her soap bubble song, as Summer labeled it in her notes. The one that shimmered and shook, floating on the breeze, without any beginning or end, just flowing around and around, in and out of itself until it faded away.

" . . . *behold the bridegroom comes in the middle of the night and we come and we come and we come to receive the light from the light that shines and shines the light from the light that shines always shines that is never overtaken by night so the light in the night and the bridegroom comes and comes and always comes in the middle of the night and blessed is the servant whom He shall find watching always watching in the gloaming and the dawning and the shining of the gladsome light in the darksome night and the wholesome shining of the light the light that gladsome light that is never overtaken by night the light that shines now now—now that we have come to the setting of the sun which burns like fire that burns through a thicket like a flame that sets the mountains on fire—the sun the Sun that shines and shines on the world is the light of wisdom the light gladsome light of wisdom for by it those who worshipped the stars were taught by a star to adore oh gladsome light that light in the night that shines and shines and behold the light of evening oh Gladsome light which burns like fire for we are consumed embraced enfolded in the fire that is love and light the light that shines and shines the light from the light oh shines always shines that is never overtaken by night darksome night the light in the night and the bridegroom comes and always comes in the middle to the night now and here and now and always and ever unto ages of ages coming and come and coming and come always and ever and Now in the night in the middle of the night and blessed is the servant whom He shall find watching always watching in the shining and the gloaming and the dawning and the shining and the light in the night and the shining of that gladsome light that is never overtaken by night but which burns through a thicket and sets the mountains on fire and behold the light of evening that is never overtaken but shines and shines for He's coming He's here He's coming to the valley of weeping and they shall walk in the light of His face which flames like fire on the mountain it shines and it shines from the mountain as much as they can bear it the light in the night on the mountain holy mountain holy fountain the fountain of light and the dove descending and Him ascending and transcending and all that is ending is starting and ending and starting and ending and always Now in the light from the light as he comes always comes in the middle of the night and blessed is the servant whom He shall find watching always watching in the shining and the gladsome light in the night and the dove which descends with the Voice that upends and the Word that descends and descends and ascends and ascends in the light from the light and behold the bridegroom comes in the middle of the night . . ."*

"That's an interesting song," Summer said, as Magda's voice faded back into silence and the cicadas' ringing. "Where did you hear it?"

"I heard it my first night in the desert."

"During your . . . exile?" Summer probed.

"Yes. That was when I heard it. It may have been a little different, but I only heard it once, and that's how I remember it."

"Tell me about your exile in the desert."

"That's a long story. It's been a long exile. Very long . . ."

"Well, maybe you can just tell me about that first day when you heard the song."

"You might be bored; it's not like a movie. But if you really want to hear it, I'll tell you."

"I do. I want to hear it," Summer said, and Magda cleared her throat as though beginning a formal oration.

***

"I awoke that morning with a headache, my mind going about its daily routine. *It's still dark*, I thought. *It must be a rainy morning. Maybe I'll wake Blaise early to have hot cocoa and watch the storm. He loves a storm. Where has Maxim gotten to? Is he already up?* These were my thoughts that first morning. I turned over, reaching out for the husband who ought to have been lying next to me. I reached, and felt, and reached farther . . . farther . . . then I fell—hard.

I lay for some time where I landed, the pain in my head still stabbing relentlessly. When I finally opened my eyes, I saw acres of sand reaching up into acres of sky, the first dotted with the heads of fierce-looking cactuses—the second slashed with the first rays of the sun bursting over a jagged mountain. I was in the desert, and I was alone . . . may I have another one of those delicious cookies you brought?"

"Of course!"

"Thank you. That was so sweet of you to bring them."

"How did you end up there . . . in the desert?" Summer asked, trying to determine how deep the logic of Magda's delusion went.

"I woke up there."

"But how did you get there initially."

"How does anyone get there initially?"

"Well, I mean, did you take a plane? A car? Did an alien starship beam you there?"

"Do you believe in aliens, Summer?" Magda looked at her skeptically and took another cookie from the box.

"Do *you*?" Summer countered.

"Why the game? I thought you wanted to know about my exile?"

"I do, I do! I'm just curious how you got to the desert in the first place. The aliens aren't important. I'm just being silly."

"Exile isn't silly—or funny."

"I know. I apologize."

"How I got there isn't important, though everyone had their theories . . . or myths, or whatever you want to call what they said."

"Who are 'they?' What myths do you mean?" Summer was beginning to suspect a lurking persecutory delusion and paranoia now.

"Well, think about it. You've heard all kinds of myths, like that camels store water in their humps or that men are anatomically short one rib, obviously, since God borrowed one from Adam to make Eve. It's just fat, you see—stored up for later. But the world is full of myths and misinformation: that war can be completely and indisputably just—that we're all destined for greatness if we only work hard enough—that the greatest good in this life is to be happy . . . and that we have a duty to pursue happiness at all cost. Or, like what people said about my exile—that I was selfish—that I didn't care about anyone else and couldn't get along—that I felt somehow responsible or guilty—that I didn't want to be happy. People think all sorts of things about exile, and hardly any of it is true. Until they face it themselves, they can't fathom why someone would go off into the desert alone."

"Wait, I thought you said you woke up there."

"I did."

"But you just made it sound like you went off into the desert on purpose."

"Well, I did, and I didn't."

"Did someone make you go?"

"Of course not. Who would have made me?"

"Well, I don't know . . . I was thinking about Napoleon, I guess."

"Napoleon? Don't think about him. It's nothing like that. How can I explain it to you? Yes, I woke up there—it's true, but over time I chose to stay, and somehow, I survived. Though Maxim and Blaise were on my mind constantly. I kept thinking about how I could get to them, but all my options were extremely dangerous, if not impossible. I simply had to wait. But in the meantime, I lived in the desert, and it has often been very hard."

"Who are Maxim and Blaise? And where did you hear the song?" Magda was quiet, watching Cat root around in the dirt with her snout, sneezing, and shaking her head so that her ears flapped like a bird.

"I suppose it wasn't really the first day when I heard it—it was the first night in the desert. I kept so busy that first day, looking for shelter . . . looking for food and drink. Keeping busy. Testing crazy plans in my head to get back to Maxim and Blaise. I guess I didn't want them to be real—so I didn't acknowledge them. I didn't want to think about them or admit they were even there. They weren't supposed to be, you know. They were supposed to disappear in the quiet of the desert."

"What was supposed to disappear?

"The voices." Summer sat forward on the bench at the mention of voices.

"Tell me more." Auditory hallucinations would be an exciting symptom. Enlightening even. This really could be schizophrenia!

"Well, there was a moment of silence at first. A living silence, not a dead one—one of peace, after my head stopped aching. I didn't notice at first. I was so busy looking for a well and something to eat. But when I finally sat down, stopped looking and thinking and planning, I heard it—or rather didn't hear it."

"What was it?"

"The silence, Summer . . . it was so absolute! It was peace. I don't remember feeling anything like it before, but I knew right away what it must be, and I wanted it to stay. I wanted it to stay forever and unto the ages of ages until the sun went cold. I could have died right then in that beautiful living silence. I was happy—weirdly and absurdly happy at my lot. I was completely alone in the desert, cut off from my family and friends with no surety of survival, and yet I had never felt such peace.

"I reveled in it once I became fully aware of it. I forgot to eat. I even forgot to look for water. I just basked in the silence. Why hadn't I come to the desert sooner? I'd been dying before, slowly but surely, minute by minute. Dying. Even before the worst day. Now I had tasted peace in the desert, and it was good!" Magda paused; a curiously serene smile spread across her face.

"That night was the first time I noticed them, you know, shining unimpeded by the lights of the city. The sky was simply thronging with stars—a spectacle I'd never seen, except in the very best of dreams. It was crowded—jostling like a busy station—all shining luminaries pushing themselves forward through the darkness. I had thought it would be like in dreams and movies where individual stars are easy to point out and even to name, but it's harder to notice individuals in such a crowded night sky. The chorus splashed its way across the dome. I think that's what they call the milky way. Of course, I'd always known they were there, but to see them! To really see them! What a gift to encounter silence and an unspoiled night sky my first night out there all alone! But how can I describe that silence? It was a silence that sang!"

"Sang?"

"Yes. I'm convinced it was the stars. They were singing, Summer. I don't know how. I didn't think they could, and I didn't know that I could hear something silent . . . and it *was* silent—so perfectly silent. How can I make it make sense to you? It's a silence that sings—it just sings, and there's no other way I can say it.

"Just imagine if everyone knew what really went on up there! We'd all be out in the desert watching and listening every night of our lives! Maybe learning how to sing along with them in that glorious living silence. It's a silence like a million songs sung simultaneously, and yet they are all somehow one and the same song. They weave in and out of each other like a dance. I wish I could write down the song I heard. I tried once. It just went on and on without end. On and on . . . All the songs and the one Song—all the voices and the one Voice. This isn't anything like it, you know . . . what I sing. But I sing it anyway, as nearly as I can imitate it, in case someday I'm delirious and forget ever having heard it . . . and in case I never hear it again . . ."

"But what about the voices?"

"The voices don't matter as much as the song."

"But I'm interested in them. What did they say?"

"I'll tell you another time. Cat's restless. It's probably time she had her dinner."

"Oh, right. She's probably hungry. I'd like to hear more of your story sometime, though. Can we talk again soon?"

"Of course. I'm sorry I ramble. I don't talk to people very much any-more. I suppose I'm a bit out of practice."

That evening, with Cat curled up by her feet snoring and occasion-ally whimpering in her sleep, Summer typed up everything she could re-member of her first real "interview" with Magda. The possible delusions, paranoia, hallucinations—the implausibility of her having ever spent time in an actual desert by herself.

For Summer, the case seemed to be leaning hard toward schizophre-nia, except that Magda seemed so lucid and organized in her telling of the story. So eloquent and well-spoken. That was the problem. Summer had read about complicated delusions before—full of convincing details and real belief in their truth—but she hadn't known or even heard of someone who seemed so simple one minute and so articulate the next. Perhaps it was dissociative identity disorder. That was incredibly rare, though—a popu-lar condition on television and in movies, but hardly ever seen in real life. She considered Occam's Razor and returned to the simplest explanation: dementia.

The thought crossed Summer's mind briefly that perhaps there was no disorder at all. Maybe Magda was simply a kooky old lady who also hap-pened to be a creative storyteller. In such a scenario, Magda might be telling the truth of her experience, but not the fact. Perhaps she was dealing with some sort of past trauma through the invention of an alternative event. Her quirks—that toothless grin and penchant for rock throwing and random comments—perhaps those were just distractions. They made a deeply com-plicated woman look simple—a sharp and incisive mind seem feeble. If this were the case, was she doing it all on purpose? And if so, why?

Many such questions troubled Summer that evening, but one more than any other: The desert, stars, and voices could all be explained one way or another, but who were Maxim and Blaise? Were they made up characters in Magda's fantasy, or did they really exist?

8

Rain in the Desert

Summer waited for what seemed an appropriate length of time before trying to interview Magda again. She was determined to wheedle out the cause of her odd behavior in the neighborhood—be it pathological or motivated by some mysterious purpose that made sense only to her. She didn't want to seem overly eager, like she wanted something from her. She hated it when she could tell someone was only paying attention to her because they wanted her to buy something or join something. She always knew it was coming, that moment when their motives became crystal clear. They weren't interested in her as a friend or even a person, but as a project or potential client. They just wanted her money or her time.

Summer told herself she wanted nothing from Magda for herself. She simply wanted to help an old woman living alone who seemed to have no one else to check up on her and make sure she was okay. That was why she had to make sure that her attentions to Magda, beyond those necessary for arranging Cat's care, seemed genuine. Because, to her mind, they obviously were.

Summer planned it all out very carefully, as usual, the day she would try to get more of Magda's exile story—more telling details and potential inconsistencies. This was surely the day she would get her to explain the voices and the pebbles.

That evening, Summer made something for Magda, rather than taking a box of store-bought cookies, even though Magda had seemed to enjoy them the last time. If she baked something herself and brought it on a real plate, it would have a more genuine, neighborly feel to it, and Magda having her plate would ensure the next encounter. Of course, growing up, Summer's parents had worked many long hours and hadn't had much time to cook. Summer hadn't learned to make much of anything from scratch as a result, but she did know how to follow directions. It didn't matter that the dough was from a plastic tube. The cookies would be warm and gooey, and that's what makes all the difference.

By that point, she knew Magda's schedule just as well as her own and could gauge the perfect timing for her visit. So as the evening closed in and the sun was low behind the trees, Summer stood in her backyard on tiptoes looking over the fence into Magda's garden. Magda was watering her tomato plants and humming to herself.

"Hello, Magda!" Summer called.

"Summer!"

"I baked cookies this afternoon. Shall I bring you some?"

"You baked them yourself?"

"I did—and they're still warm!"

"Yes, yes—come over and sit for a while." Summer clipped on Cat's leash and picked up the attractively arranged plate of cookies.

"Don't pull, no! You'll make me drop them! Catherine! No pulling!" When Cat knew where they were going, she wasted no time getting there, straining against her collar, wheezing and coughing all the way to Magda's gate. Summer, meanwhile, kept a precarious hold on her plate of strategic cookies.

"Oh, don't those look tasty!" Magda's lips spread in her sparsely toothed grin as she leaned in, smelling the cookies, still warm on the plate.

"I hope you like chocolate chip."

"Of course! Come sit with me for a while. I thought I might see you sooner, but I suppose you've been very busy with school lately?"

"Yes, I suppose I have been. Lots to do. Lots to read. How was your week?" Summer asked.

"Much like any other," Magda chuckled. "You are the only variation in my life these days. It's nice to have a conversation sometimes with questions you don't expect."

"What do you mean?"

"Oh, you know . . . every day Mr. Eberly across the street says it's a nice day, no matter the weather, when I pass him getting into his car on the way to his office. Then Mrs. Turnipseed—isn't that an excellent name? I love her name so much! Every day after Mr. Eberly says it's a nice day and pulls out of his driveway, Mrs. Turnipseed comes out with her Pomeranian and asks if I'll be around to weed at the usual time, and I say yes. The mailman comes while I weed Mr. Eastman's yard, and he always says something about working hard and making sure I drink enough water. So, you see? You are the most unpredictable part of my life now. I never know what you'll ask me next."

"I do ask a lot of questions. I'm sorry. I hope it's not too much."

"Well, I do think it's my turn to ask you a few," Magda said, slyly eyeing the plate of cookies before reaching for a second.

"Of course! What would you like to know?"

"Why do you want to leave the desert?" Magda asked.

"Oh . . . well, growing up, I'd always read books and seen movies about places with lots of rain and trees and forests. It seemed so much more alive, you know. Like the landscape wasn't trying its hardest to kill you! And that's how it sometimes felt, as a kid. It's just so forbidding, especially in the summer."

"And you want to be comfortable?"

"Yeah, I suppose you could put it that way. My skin got awfully dry there."

"You were parched, no doubt. I know the feeling. Like you could drink for hours and still be thirsty."

"Well, maybe. I mean, we're definitely careful not to waste water in Albuquerque. I remember I used to be so excited if it rained, though. It was like a present just for me! I used to sit by the window and watch it fall, then go outside and just smell it—smell the air. There's a smell after a rain in the desert that I can't really describe, but it's wonderful."

"Yes, rain in the desert is very special. Precious."

"You've seen it?"

"Seen it? Oh, yes—I've seen it." Magda got a far off look in her eyes, and Summer knew more of her desert exile delusion was forthcoming.

"Tell me about it."

"Well, it was when you talked about the smell that I remembered the first time it rained during my exile. I could smell it coming well before it arrived, you know. It was autumn, I think. Yes, it was definitely autumn though you wouldn't have known it by the heat. The temperature hadn't dipped—the sun still scorched my skin—the air still seared my nostrils with every breath. I couldn't be out at midday. I was still weak and couldn't yet bear it. Still, I noticed a change in the air, mostly in the way it looked: The color of the light and its angle as it touched the distant mountaintops.

"I had long since lost my sense of time—my sense of season. I had no calendar in my cave to mark the important days: the feasts and fasts and controversial civic celebrations. The sun and falling fruit were my only clues that Advent was coming. Well, no—there were other clues as well. Certain birds started showing up whom I never saw except around the Winter Pascha.

"Only the toughest birds stay in the desert throughout the Lenten months when food and water are scarce—the wakeful, watchful hours long. The Cactus Wren, the Cooper's Hawk, the black Phainopepla, its red eye flashing among the mistletoe berries where it holds vigil. These, the ascetics and stylites of the avian class.

"I remember the day—the promise of approaching rain. I remember I decided to harvest the mesquite. Better to get it slightly early than slightly (or very) wet. I found a wash not far from my cave that was overgrown with mesquite. I planned to harvest more than I needed to have a little more security come winter. It's supposed to keep well, you know, it has some protein, and the taste isn't bad. The mesquites were heavy with pods. They weren't falling yet, but they came off easily, so they were ripe enough. I got started harvesting in the morning before the sun rose and finished before my skin started burning. I rescued quite a lot of it before the rain came."

"You ate mesquite pods?"

"Well, I processed them. Ground them with stones into a sort of meal."

"What else did you eat?"

"Oh, there's a lot of food in the desert if you know where to look for it, and it's a good thing too since I ended up losing most of my mesquite. It was only a matter of time before I had a burglar."

"A burglar?"

Yes—a rat. It got into my mesquite while I was sleeping. Thankfully, the desert has something to eat in all seasons because some of my stores spoiled when rain leaked in, and more of it was stolen by the rat. The barrel cactuses saved me when my stores were gone—the tart, fleshy fruits but especially the mild, fatty seeds. At first, I just ate them raw, which was fine. Eventually, I found that lightly toasting them over the fire was good. I wouldn't necessarily give them five stars . . . well, maybe. I suppose it depends on your standards and what you compare them to! But I remember liking them and wishing Blaise and Maxim could try my desert foods."

"Tell me about Blaise and Maxim," Summer said, seeing a chance to ask about the two central characters whose existence she doubted. Magda was silent, examining her hands as they lay clasped on her lap.

"I'll tell you about them some time. Maybe when you're ready to tell me about Catherine."

"Catherine . . . my dog?"

"No, the one you named the dog after." Summer's heart started thumping rapidly. Her scalp began to burn, and she felt a little dizzy. She took a deep breath and let it out slowly. How had Magda guessed about Catherine?

"Well, you're right," Summer said at last. "I did name her after someone. I'll let you know when I'm ready to talk about her. I'm not quite there yet."

"I understand. I can wait. I trust you can too." Magda laid her shriveled hand on Summer's and squeezed.

"Of course," Summer said. She had been thrown off by Magda asking her about Catherine. Still, she quickly pulled herself together and continued questioning Magda about her exile, testing the consistency and degree of detail in her story. "Well, I know what you mean about knowing rain is coming before it actually arrives. The smell is half the pleasure of a rain in the desert. Did you see quite a few storms?"

"Yes, I remember one storm in particular—that day after harvesting the mesquite. It was a sweltering afternoon. I was in my cave cataloging my food stores, and in that confined space, I smelled something horrible! I couldn't escape it, no matter where I went. I couldn't escape it because it was me! Ha! Try as you might, it's impossible to escape yourself. I stank. I didn't know it was even possible to smell that bad. It's not as though I could spare the water to bathe or clean my clothes. I thought maybe during the next rainstorm, I would strip and leave my clothes out in it—maybe get a cold shower myself.

"It's funny, isn't it," Magda continued, "considering how we live here and now. I had just never known a human being could smell so bad. We wash a lot, I suppose and cover our stink with pleasant scents. Under all that, I think it's our reality—our condition to stink and to be ashamed of it. We humans really are an embarrassed bunch. Maybe that's what makes us so easy to manipulate and control.

"Our shame makes us desperate to hide—to cover our embarrassing bodies with the newest fashions—to cover up the stench of impending death with the latest fragrances. We cover up and hide all our secret and shameful doings in the newest and nicest and cleanest homes (or caves—yes, even in the desert, there's the temptation to keep up with imaginary Joneses). We just loathe ourselves, don't we! All we do is hide what we really are. We hide, and we pretend. And we try to make more money so we can afford to hide and pretend more comfortably and stylishly."

"Do you hate yourself, Magda?" Summer asked, poised to quote some pithy nuggets of pseudo-wisdom about self-care and self-love. Magda just laughed.

"Not anymore."

"You got your shower, then? Did it help your self-esteem?"

"Self-esteem? I'm not sure that's how I would put it . . . but it's true I never realized how embarrassed I was until I was naked in the middle of the desert—smelling wretched—no other human to see me or smell me but embarrassed nonetheless. Just waiting for the rain to start. It's not just the stink, though, you know. No makeup to enhance what I had always considered my strong points or to hide what I'd rather conceal. My filthy and far from fashion-forward clothes hung up on a Palo Verde waiting, like me, for the shower to finally come.

"I was just standing there naked and silly-looking—waiting—and naked people aren't sexy, Summer. You know how naked people are supposed to be sexy, or we're supposed to think they are? Well, they're not. They're shocking for two seconds, and then they're just silly, floppy, and a bit absurd. But why should I have cared? I think we do all this deceptive grooming and fumigating and costuming to convince everyone else that we aren't silly or stinky or hideous. But who was there to impress? I was so utterly alone."

"Well, you wanted to feel good about yourself, for your own sake, didn't you? And there's nothing wrong with that—in fact, I would say it's very well-adjusted to care more about your own self-opinion than anyone else's. It's important to cultivate a sort of acceptance of yourself by taking the time to care for yourself physically and emotionally. Effective self-care helps you maintain a healthy relationship with yourself, you know? That's what self-love is, really. A healthy relationship with yourself. Even when we're alone, we need to feel good about ourselves, right? Not for everyone else, but for us."

"Yes . . . yes, I think you may be right. We do want to feel good about ourselves, but why? Maybe we don't do all this just to impress others but prove to ourselves as much as everyone else that we're actually different.

We're special. We're uniquely animate, sentient, and real in a world full of dirty, inanimate, in-sentient, sub-reality. We're better than all that. Everything and everyone else is slightly (or sometimes extremely) less real than we are. We're embarrassed for them but secretly triumphant that we do 'being human' so much better than they do. After all, we never stink like that or do and say silly things in front of others. We work very hard to be real and, above all, not to be embarrassed."

"That's not what I . . . I mean, I don't know that I would—"

"We do, Summer! Look, we try so hard to rise above it all, and still, this is what we return to! We're stinky, shocking, flawed, fractured, and utterly dislocated from what is real. The more we try to seem real, the less real we become. And should someone actually edge nearer to reality, we pity them! How embarrassed they must feel right now! After all, that's how we would feel! Madness! Madness to stop caring—to stop trying to be seen to advantage! Madness to let yourself be seen for the tired, ugly, stinky mess that you are! Madness to look for a cure beyond bubble baths and affirmational mantras repeated into a mirror."

Summer was taken aback. The more Magda talked, the less simpleminded she seemed. Though she smiled with her jack-o-lantern teeth and reached slyly for more cookies and threw rocks at houses, Magda's turn of thought and phrase was quite simply shocking in its range and depth. Disordered it may be, but simple it was not.

"Are you real, Magda?" She finally said, looking askance at her neighbor.

"What do you think?"

"I don't know what I think . . . I don't even know what I mean. Never mind. Did you get your shower at last?"

"I did, finally, and it was frigid. But I knew it didn't really solve anything. Not really. I stopped stinking for an hour or two, and then I started to stink again. Maybe that's part of the embarrassment. How soon after getting cleaned up, we're dirty and stinky again. It's hopeless! We're just messy, and it will take a different kind of bath to really clean us. One that would get to the root cause. Maybe wash away the embarrassment and shame as well. But you know, I think it's right that we're embarrassed to smell like death. We do, and it's horrible, and it feels like it shouldn't be like that because it shouldn't. Even now, I'm like a walking corpse. And I feel I have been for a long time, even back when I didn't smell like an old lady."

"You don't smell bad, Magda. And I'm sure you have nothing to feel ashamed of. You need to stop telling yourself rude things—you should only ever talk to yourself the way you would talk to a precious loved one. If you wouldn't say it to a little child, you shouldn't say it to yourself. You must love yourself, Magda. Love yourself first and foremost, and everything else will make sense after that." Magda looked at Summer with something like amusement.

"What would you rather be, Summer? A unicorn or a pegasus?"

9

Autumn

As the days grew increasingly shorter and relatively cooler, Summer finally built a real fire in her fireplace. With plenty of trial and error and internet searches, she learned the lessons of ancient humanity and produced fire, albeit with several boxes of matches and crumpled newspapers. Come November, most of her evenings were spent by a crackling blaze with Cat asleep on her feet and Magda's case file on her lap. Five months of observation and informal interviews had brought her no closer to a diagnosis but only raised more questions. Still, Summer kept daily records of Magda's comings and goings and doings, and still, she speculated about root causes of Magda's delusions and abnormal behaviors.

One crisp Saturday morning, Summer came to Magda with a loaf of homemade bread. Summer had discovered that fall that she liked baking and set herself the goal of learning to bake her own bread. The dense, somewhat crumbly loaf she took to Magda that morning was still hot from the oven. Summer always brought baked goods when she wanted Magda to talk. In her own experience, food was comforting and made words flow more freely from the heart, especially when that heart was bruised or broken. Magda spread her lips in her usual birdshot grin and automatically sat Summer down in their accustomed spot under the apple tree, now harvested of its fruits.

"I have something for you, too," Magda said as she reached into one of her deep skirt pockets and pulled out a jar. "I made it yesterday from the apples. It's applesauce."

"Oh, how nice! Thank you!"

"It's a treat to have in the fall. Maybe you can put it in your oatmeal."

"That sounds nice. I'll try it."

"I'm doing my pumpkins next."

"You eat them? They're not just for decoration?"

"Of course not—nothing is just for decoration. Pumpkins are very wholesome. I'll give you some when it's ready."

"It must be nice for you to have such a productive garden—I mean, after the austerity of your exile . . ." Summer said casually, trying to tempt another story.

"Yes, it is productive—a very lively garden. It's my privilege to care for it. Yes . . . very lively."

"Not like the desert . . . we could never have a garden like this in Albuquerque."

"Not like this one, no. But the desert has its own life—severe though it may be," Magda said. Summer was silent. Through her few clinical observations that semester, she had learned that silence was often more effective than too many questions in encouraging a patient to confide. And so, she waited, watching an equally patient Eastern Phoebe perched on the fence post hawking for small insects. After a moment, Magda took the bait and began.

"At any one time in the desert, it feels as though life is precarious. In the scorching summer, there are those plants that thrive and those that appear to die. In the cool of winter, the balance seems to reverse. Things long thought dead heave a sigh of relief, springing back to life, and those that had been looking so vital and equal to the harsh environment, appear in their turn to waste away. It looks like the desert is always somewhere between living and dying. Even some saguaros, which seem so stalwart in every season, will sometimes look half dead. They actually are, though. I've seen what looks like a blackened, dead stump with a living arm stretching out of it up to the sky. An impossible living appendage growing from a rotting cadaver that might at any moment collapse under it. Strange."

"I've seen things like that, too," Summer said.

"It's common. We're all a bit like that, aren't we? But even with the cycle of birth and death playing out through the seasons, some elements are so vital! I don't think I've ever been as alive as they are."

"What do you mean? What elements?"

"The birds."

"Birds?"

"Yes, like the Cactus Wren. Going about its business perfectly comfortable with the harshness of its neighborhood. It's so fully alive sitting on a half-dead cactus or leafless skeleton—it rests happy enough among the brutal spines. They remind me of a picture I once saw of a Hindu yogi from long ago lounging on a bed of spikes," Magda said with a grin.

"You did say the desert birds are the ascetics of the winged world," Summer joked.

"So they are! They've learned the delicate art of needing very little . . . of living contentedly amongst the spines. Or maybe the spines have grown up around them to protect their nests. Maybe the cactuses enjoy their tenants and kindly protect them from intruders."

"What came first, the cactus or the wren?" Summer asked with a laugh.

"I wonder the same," Magda said in a low, serious tone. "Was the desert made for them, or were they made for the desert? I felt alien in it, myself—like an invasive species. I wondered if I could ever become a part of the desert landscape and belong in it like the Cactus Wren. To be at home in the heat, the dust, and the spines and actually feel thankful for it."

"But why should you? You're not a Cactus Wren. You're a gardener, Magda." Magda looked at Summer with a sense of astonishment Summer hadn't expected. They both returned to silence and watched the hawking Phoebe return to its fence post. "I mean . . . why be in the desert at all if you don't have to be? What's it all for?" Summer asked, still watching the bird.

"We're all in the desert, Summer. Some of us just don't realize it."

"Do you often . . . do you sometimes feel like all of this . . . this life isn't real? Like maybe you're watching your life from the outside?" Summer asked, testing a theory.

"Sweet girl, you're young and strong. Do you like to climb trees?" Magda asked suddenly. Summer took three slow deep breaths, remembering how long it took her to get over the pony comment . . . then the unicorn and pegasus. Magda just said these things. She wasn't well. It wasn't that she was deliberately trying to make Summer feel like a child and poking at her insecurities. She was disordered. Nothing she said could be taken too seriously. Summer cleared her throat.

"Honestly, Magda, I haven't climbed a tree since I was a child. That was so very long ago now that I'm afraid I've forgotten how." Summer was satisfied with that answer. It sounded mature.

"Oh, that's a shame. I don't think I can manage it this year. I've fallen before, and now my old bones don't heal as fast. Shame . . ."

"What do you mean, Magda?"

"Oh, it's just that I have a beautiful old pecan tree on the other side of the house, and it's ready to harvest. I think it's going to rain tomorrow, so I was hoping to shake the nuts down today."

"You actually climb up there and shake them down?" Summer asked in amazement as she pointed toward the towering old pecan tree whose canopy rose high above the rooftop.

"Well, they fall on their own over a few months, and every day I pick up what I find. But I can gather more at once if I spread a few big sheets under the tree, climb up there, and shake them down. I suppose I could try it again—maybe you could wait for me at the bottom to help me in case I fall . . ."

"You know what, Magda? I think I'll make an exception just this once and climb that tree for you."

***

There was a particular tree in Summer's neighborhood park growing up. Its tiny leaves grew along the stem's shaft like a feather, and in the summertime, it had puffy pink fairy blossoms. Her mother called it a Mimosa tree. It was not a native, and Summer knew no other tree like it. It was so full of friendly personality, Summer called it *her* tree.

The first time Summer climbed this particular tree, she couldn't get back down. She called her father over from the park bench, crying for help, but to her astonishment and despair, he wouldn't pick her up and rescue her. Such betrayal! Why would he not save her? Instead, her father stood under the tree, telling her where to step next until she was finally reunited with solid ground. Having thus made the journey down the tree on her own, the tree truly became hers.

After that day, Summer often returned to her tree's friendly branches to read a book, to think, or pretend she was a bird or a squirrel or a bee in one of its Suessical blooms. She talked to the tree and told it about her day. She told it about how lonely she felt, and it listened. She told it about Catherine, and it held her. But that was all long ago, and Summer had never loved another tree as she had loved that one.

Summer loved all trees hypothetically, but not personally, as a friend and confidant. Now, as Summer stood under Magda's towering old pecan tree, a ladder leaned up against its trunk, she felt the strange urge to introduce herself before she climbed it—ask its permission before she made so bold as to grip its arms and shake them.

Magda had spread a few old sheets under the branches like a vast dingy Christmas tree skirt, then stood well back in expectation of fallout. Summer took a deep breath and began to climb. It all came back, those summer days alone in her tree, dreaming—wishing—the day in middle school when she decided she was too mature for tree-climbing. A bitter-sweet nostalgia washed over her as she remembered, then she carefully stepped onto one of the thicker boughs and began, gently at first, to bounce. A few nuts plopped to the ground.

"Don't be timid—it's a tough old tree. You can shake it a bit harder," Magda shouted up to her, a wrinkled hand upheld to block the sun's glare.

Summer shook, bounced, and jostled—laughing at how much she enjoyed it—feeling a childlike satisfaction from the plunking sound as the nuts hit the ground. Magda laughed, too. She sat with her buckets, watching Summer forget she was a medical student—watching her forget about that oppressive need to always be mature and professional. Cat ran back and forth, barking up at the tree, and at Summer.

"Catherine, look! I'm a squirrel!" The dog howled up at Summer, and she howled back down at Cat as the nuts came tumbling down. When Summer finally came back to earth, still laughing, her cheeks glowed pink like fall apples.

"Well done, Summer! Now you can help me pick them up!" Magda handed her a bucket. "Leave the ones that've been chewed on in a heap to the side. There's plenty for everyone." Summer and Magda combed the grass for nuts that had fallen outside of the sheets' radius, filling buckets with pounds and pounds of pecans.

"Wow!" Summer wiped her brow as she surveyed the buckets of nuts. "Can I try one?" She held up one of the green husks and shook it by her ear, listening as the pecan thumped around inside.

"Of course you can! But there's a lot of work to do before then. We have a few, like that one, still in their husks. Careful. They can turn your fingers black."

"Really? But they're green!"

"Yes, really. Would you like to help me process them? If you've never done it, it could be interesting for you . . . and it is a lot of work for one little old lady." Magda winked mischievously.

"I guess I have the time," Summer said, glancing at her watch. "Just tell me what to do."

"Well, let's get off any remaining husks. We don't need those. Here, wear my gloves. I don't mind if my fingers go black." Summer pulled on the pair of stiff old gardening gloves, which had an odd musty smell about them, and which were too big for either of them. "Now, see? They're already started; you can just pry it the rest of the way open with a knife—here. That's right. It's easy. While you work on that, I'll go make a fire."

"A fire?" Summer asked, a bit alarmed. "Where? What for?"

"In the fire pit. I always do it outside. Can you imagine trying to boil that many nuts in the kitchen?" She laughed at the thought and began throwing dry branches into a shallow pit circled with rocks.

"Wait, but why are we boiling them?"

"It'll help loosen the shells."

Summer tried to focus on her job, scoring the green husks and pealing them from the smooth, brown shells inside. Magda had started a raging blaze in her little fire pit, and sparks flew like fireflies from the pile of crackling branches. When the fire started burning down a bit and forming coals, Magda stood an iron rack over the pit, heaving an enormous stockpot on top of it. Then she hauled over the garden hose and filled the pot with water.

"Got all the husks off? Good! Now, while we wait for the water to boil, let's sort out the bad nuts."

"How can you tell if it's bad?"

"Look for cracks and holes. Feel each one and check to see if any feel too light. Give them a little shake to see if any of them rattle."

"You want a bit of a rattle?"

"No. Don't keep the ones that rattle. Put the bad nuts in this pile."

Having sorted through the first bucket of nuts, Magda tossed the good ones into the boiling water and the bad ones onto her compost heap. Then they began sorting the next bucket, and in that fashion, boiled each batch of pecans. While the last batch was boiling, Magda showed Summer a strange looking device with a lever. Placing one of the boiled nuts inside, she pulled the lever, squeezing the nut until the shell cracked. Magda's fingers worked nimbly at the broken bits of shell, and the end product was two perfect pecan halves.

"Ooo, can we taste it now?"

"Well, we could, but it'll be better toasted, and they will keep better that way, too. Here, you can crack them, and I'll shell them. If you get ahead of me, you can shell some too. Put the meats in the bowl, but make sure they are absolutely picked clean first."

Summer had blisters on her hands and sore, red fingers by the time all the nuts were shelled. Evening was closing in, and it occurred to her that they had worked all day and hadn't eaten or taken a rest. She rubbed her sore hands and watched as Magda, seemingly inexhaustible, built up the fire again and placed a wide skillet on the rack over the flames. She shook a layer of nuts into the pan, and as the roasting nuts began to sweat and smell sweet, Summer realized how hungry she had become from their labor. Each batch of toasted nuts was then transferred to a basket to cool, then into large jars in which they would be sealed the next day. When the last batch was stowed, Magda smiled broadly and held out a little handful of toasted nuts. Summer ate the still-warm pecans slowly. Never had she worked so hard for food in her life, nor had she ever eaten anything so satisfying.

10

The Birds

Summer and Magda sat on the bench under the apple tree that fall evening, wrapped in warm sweaters, eating Summer's loaf of bread and
sharing a bowl of the warm toasted pecans. For once, Summer had no questions and simply sat in the wordless glow of satisfaction over their day's
work. Magda's face had an uncharacteristically serious shade about it as she
stared at the old house in front of her.

"You know, Summer," she began, without shifting her gaze, "exile
doesn't have to be painful. It's only painful when you can't fully detach
yourself from certain old loves . . . and my exile has been painful."

"What do you mean?"

"I can renounce things. I have renounced them . . . but I still care too
much. I've made a little progress. Detached myself from many things, many
loves, many needs, in fact. But one thing remains—just one thing—one big
thing. I can't seem to let it go. I edge away. I look at other things. But it's so
big, it's hard to stop looking at it. It's hard to leave something so significant
behind. I fear someday it may have to be taken away from me by force,
though maybe that would be for the best." Magda finally examined Summer's face thoughtfully.

Summer was confused. She was often confused when Magda talked of
exile, but she had learned to be quiet over the past few weeks and just listen.
She had learned something about the old woman. When she spoke of the
desert—when she spoke of her exile—she was speaking another language.
She was talking in poetry—an elaborate cipher that required interpretation. What she needed was a key—some means of translating the code. That

was it—Magda spoke in code. Whether purposefully or not, whether from years spent alone, quiet with her thoughts, perhaps owing to some residual influence of her formal education, she had developed a poetical account of her life.

Summer listened, often trying to assign possible one-to-one connections, as though the desert exile were some sort of allegorical tale. She searched for the lesson, the story within the story, but often became so immersed in the telling of it that she half-believed this odd old woman to have really lived in a desert, foraging for food, and living in a cave. She almost wanted to believe it—no, not almost. She *did* want to believe it with all her heart. There was a beauty to the story—a roundness, and fullness, and mystery that appealed to her in a way she couldn't quite put her finger on. It was as if this alien experience was something they shared. As though Magda recounted not only her own past but Summer's too. They lived it together. They suffered the heat and dry together. They searched for the deep, desert wells hand in hand. Summer and Magda were in the desert together, somehow, inexplicably bound to each other—strangers across time and realities.

It bothered Summer. It bothered her logical mind. It bothered her practical and tangible idea of life and how it is lived. But she couldn't quite shake the feeling that every time Magda spoke of her exile, a dense fog began to clear. Just as one's brain fills the gaps and missing information within the ambiguity of fog—fills it with shapes and colors to make sense of the emptiness—that fog took the form of everything she clung to as real. As Magda's story blew through her mind, and those certainties began to fade, Summer began to glimpse something stretching before her in all directions—a vast, howling desert. She felt its heat—its reality. Surely Magda was just an uncommonly talented storyteller.

"Do you remember the birds?" Magda asked. Summer nodded, drifting pensively to the sound of Magda's voice and feeling content with her bread and nuts.

"They sat in the cactus spines," Summer said. "I remember."

"Yes. When you're all alone, you notice these things. You notice the personalities of birds. Their society and way of life pass unnoticed when you're busy playing at life in the habited lands, but it is a parallel world full of its own dramas and disputes. Family tensions—fledgling rebellions—bad manners, and sibling rivalries. The grating, rasping squawk of the cactus wren as it noses about the bark of some tree or clump of brush for insects. The Northern Mockingbird showing off its flexible range from some great height, like a classical tenor on stage, awaiting the roses and applause following his rendition of *Nessun Dorma*." Summer laughed. She wouldn't have known what *Nessun Dorma* was if it hadn't been for her music appreciation course as an undergraduate. She liked the idea of a bird as an operatic tenor.

"Someone, long ago, brought lovebirds to the Sonoran Desert from the African continent. Sometimes I would hear them yelling their most ugly screeches and look up to see their sweet peachy faces snuggling up to one another. It's unfortunate that such beautiful, colorful birds should sound so ugly. I guess they must sound beautiful to each other, or else they constantly envy the Mockingbird his tremendous voice—but I don't get that impression. They seem to be content and affectionate birds who just happen to be tone-deaf. Or maybe I am—who's to say? I would look at them and remember Maxim."

"Tell me about Maxim," Summer said. Magda just smiled and shook her head.

"I wanted so badly to befriend them, the birds. I thought maybe I wouldn't be so terribly lonely if they would come and visit with me sometimes. Most of all, I wanted the quail to like me. I admired their sweet little family units! I liked the Gambels' funny, wobbly feather headpieces! They looked so grand and prim like they were going to high tea at a fancy hotel. They just had that look, as though they would surely know which fork to use . . ." Magda drifted off in thought, staring at something far away.

"And did you?"

"Did I . . . ?"

"Make friends with the birds."

"It's complicated."

"Really? Making friends with birds?" Summer laughed incredulously.

"Well, think about it: Humans are hard enough to befriend, and we are the same species, speaking the same language, at least for the most part. What makes animals different from people?"

"Lots of things . . . I mean, they're animals."

"But what keeps us from being friends with them easily?" Summer shrugged. "Well, animals don't usually trust people, Summer. They know that we can and usually do, want the wrong things—things that can hurt them . . . and ourselves. So, in order to bear one's soul to a bird and become friends, one must show them that one's intentions are, in fact, pure, like theirs are. So, I asked myself: Are my intentions pure? I think so . . . I don't want to hurt them. I just want to make a connection with another living thing. I don't want to feel alone. There's nothing wrong with that, right?"

"Right."

"Well, I settled on offering gifts as a token of my goodwill. I had to figure out what they might like—they want very little in life. Food seemed like the natural answer, so I observed them to see what they liked best to eat."

"And what was that?" Summer asked.

"Based on my observations, quail ate seeds. That much was clear. It was harder to determine which seeds were their special favorites that might be considered a decadent treat as opposed to nourishing yet somewhat loathsome staple." Summer laughed. She was often delighted and surprised by Magda's clever turn of phrase, which seemed to come so effortlessly.

"So, what did you do?"

"Well, I gathered a good variety of seeds and put them out for the quail. I decided to retreat to a safe distance, then come back before they'd finished to inspect their leftovers. My guess was that they would probably eat their favorites first, so the leftovers should betray their preferences. Unless they saved their favorites for dessert, in which case I would have had it backward. But I went with my suspicion that birds were most like children who eat their favorites first. In this way, I would determine which seeds to gather again and which ones to stop bothering with. A good experiment, right?"

"Sounds like it."

"Wrong. It was a bad experiment."

"Oh."

"I had to do it all over again, controlling for birds outside my sample population coming in and skewing my data. Use your head, Summer."

"Um . . ."

"But how could I keep the other birds from swooping in?"

"I . . . well, I really couldn't say."

"Observation, observation, observation! An ethnography of the quail. A qualitative analysis of their habits."

"Qualitative?" Summer asked, playing dumb to see what Magda knew.

"Yes, you know. Like what you do with me."

"What? I don't . . ." Summer blushed. How did Magda know? The old woman just laughed.

"So I started my quail ethnography, observing their haunts and habits, keeping records and observations, trying not to make any premature assumptions."

"And what kind of pattern did you observe?"

"They frequently visited certain mesquite thickets, often at certain times. It was there and then that I left my seed mix."

"And did it work?"

"It did. I replicated a few times with the same result each time. I had my answer."

"Which was?"

"They weren't terribly picky eaters. Largely vegetarian. They liked the mistletoe berries quite well. It was those I chose as my gift of pure friendship." Magda got one of those faraway looks she often got when she was telling a story. It was never clearly evident to Summer whether she had lost her place, was thinking about what to say next, or had become so lost in her own thoughts that she forgot she wasn't alone in her garden.

"So . . . were you able to win them over?"

"Win them over?" Magda asked dreamily.

"Yeah—gain their trust—make them your friends."

"Oh, yes. In a manner of speaking." She trailed off again. A slight mist came over her crinkled eyes, and she sighed. "I think that's enough about the birds."

They sat in silence for a while until Summer couldn't contain her question any longer. It was a question she had held inside for a while, not wanting to offend.

"Tell me something, Magda—" Summer paused; there seemed no better time to ask. Magda heaved a sigh as if regretting the interrupted silence. "Tell me . . . did you ever go to college?" Magda didn't look at Summer but rose from the bench and knelt down by her cabbage bed. Had Magda not heard? Was she offended by Summer's question? Magda dug at the soil with her fingers, loosening the roots of weeds that were starting to encroach on her cabbages. Summer waited, then attempted to justify her curiosity. "Only the way you talk . . . you talk like someone who's done an awful lot of reading." Magda plucked a few insects from the shiny, bald cabbage heads, stuck them in her little pillbox, then paused, looking up at the darkening November sky.

"You don't have to go to college to read a lot," she finally said.

"No, I suppose not. So . . . you didn't?"

"I did."

"Really?"

"Yes. A long time ago." She chuckled softly. "A very long time ago!"

"Tell me about it. Where did you go? What did you study?"

"I went to a women's college close to here. I studied English litera-ture—to be a teacher, you know. That's what women did back then. Not like you. You can do anything with yourself. Things have changed. It's good—a good change."

"And did you? Teach, I mean?"

"For a while. I didn't really want to teach—to be in charge of a class-room and try to make learning happen. I just wanted to read the books. So many good books. I read a lot for a long time."

"What about now?"

"Oh, I remember them. I don't need to read them again. They served their purpose. It was time to move on."

"But . . . why did you stop? There are always more books. You can't have read them all!"

"No, it's true, there are always more books, but I read the important ones. After a while, it's just a distraction."

"Distraction! From what?"

"From now."

"Gardening?"

"No, from right now—the moment. I don't want to fail to attend the moment. I've missed enough of them already. You can't go back, you know. There will always be that moment you failed to attend when maybe you missed something that could have changed everything. To make that meet-ing. God is always with us—here—in the present moment. We can be atten-tive and stay with Him, or we can distract ourselves with other things. He doesn't leave, you know. We do. We leave."

"You believe in God, Magda?" Summer asked. Magda just laughed.

"Is nothing real to you, Summer? Is the garden a figment of your imagination? The scent of the decomposing leaves and the soil? Are you a disembodied spirit, and am I some absurd voice you've made up to talk to because you're lonely? Do you have to examine everything with a micro-scope to believe it exists? I'm too big, sweet girl. I won't fit on a slide or on an agar plate, so how could God? What do you do with things too big to see? What do you do with mystery? Things for which there is no vocabu-lary—no textbook—no reference point. What do you do with the things you can't explain? Reduce them to a classification? A diagnosis? Something that can be explained and treated?"

"No, of course not! Don't be unjust, Magda! I don't do that at all!"

"No? You don't dissect the things that don't make sense to you? Try to label them, categorize them, so you can fix them if they don't fit your understanding of what's normal and healthy? So you can cope with uncertainty and mystery?"

Summer's face burned. She wanted to snap back that she was a professional. She would never make a diagnosis about "fixing" a person's essence—that which makes them unique—just because she was different or didn't understand it. And she didn't have to understand everything. She was more open-minded than that. She understood the danger of a reductionist view of personality—the danger of letting her own personal biases influence her professional evaluations. She'd written an ethics paper on the topic only last year. She breathed deep the lavender oil on her wrist.

"I just want to help people who are hurting, Magda. I can't change them—I wouldn't want to change them even if I could." Summer said this with a tone of patient condescension, having composed herself enough to put on her clinical voice. "Are you hurting? Do you need my help? You know you can always talk to me about anything." Magda smiled.

"I fear you are too kind—too accommodating to give me the help I need. But don't feel bad. I don't need you to take away my pain. I don't need you to explain it to me either. I do hope one of these days to help you . . . to help you to understand your own pain and realize my desert stories are your stories too. They're our stories—yours and mine. We're in exile together, and I know sometimes you feel it too. I've seen you go there, briefly, to the very edge. But it scares you, not only because it's a place you've convinced yourself doesn't exist, but because all this time you've been trying to solve something about *me* . . . ignoring the fact that you're the one dying of thirst . . . and I'm trying . . . I'm trying to show you where to find a well because I've been here for many years. I've been here much longer than you have, sweet girl. I can help you if you let me. It can be beautiful, the desert, if you accept that you're in it before it kills you."

"You must be thinking of Albuquerque, where I grew up. It's a real place on a map. I've never been in your desert, Magda."

"You have, though. You're in it right now."

"I'm in your garden. I'm under the apple tree, like always. I'm not in the desert, Magda. Neither are you. In fact, I don't believe you ever have been." Summer said this with hesitation, fearing what effect this statement might have on the fragile fabric of Magda's delusion. Could she accept it? Would she be angry or incredulous to have her delusion challenged? But the old woman's face showed no distress or anger. Her eyes crinkled in the smile that showed her missing teeth. She took Summer's hand in her own warm one—blackened with soil and pecan husks, rough with callouses. She looked into Summer's eyes in the growing dusk, and Summer felt like a child receiving a lesson—not a rebuke, but some loving truth about growing up.

"Ours is a desert more real than your Albuquerque. More real than the Mojave or the Sonoran or the Sahara or the Gobi. I woke up here and knew quite well where I was because I was a grownup and had lived a little. I knew this place—not because of maps and documentaries and pictures from the National Geographic. It's a place spoken about in hushed tones. Mentioned with dread by those who don't know it but have heard stories or seen what it has done to others without really understanding it. Perhaps they've seen the ones who didn't survive but lost their minds trying to find a way out—or worse yet, took the forbidden exit . . .

"You poor, poor child! Perhaps you don't even remember what it's like not to be here—not to be all dried out, wind-whipped, and thirsty. It was so long ago that you arrived. You fell from a beautiful little child-sized asteroid, like the prince in the story. You landed in this desert and are looking for a friend because you don't know you should be looking for a well. Old Magda will be your friend. And I will help you find what you aren't looking for, too. Help you break through the pain and experience the beauty of the desert—its thronging silence. The song of the stars! I never thought to meet anyone else here or to take on a novice. I still feel like such a novice myself. But you fell from the sky into my corner of the desert, so what else can I do? Don't you fret, sweet girl. Old Magda's going to help you."

11

The Weight of Love

Winter came, and with it, Summer's break from medical school. Perhaps it was the free time—the moments with nothing else to worry about. No deadlines. No papers. No research. No clinical observation. Only Cat—and Summer loved her, showering her with constant affection. Her love for the dog was heavy, fatiguing, fraught with anxiety for both of them. Summer fussed over every little thing—Cat's diet down to the daily calorie count and nutritional breakdown—and called the vet's office regularly just in case any slight change in Cat might be indicative of serious illness.

Cat's fur was thin and fine. She didn't have a double coat—that warm, downy layer of fluff under a layer of guard hairs, like a retriever or a husky. Somewhere in her unique blended heritage, Cat had inherited a smooth single coat, which meant that Summer didn't have to deal with profuse biannual shedding. It also meant that Cat was sensitive to the cold. The first time Summer saw Cat shiver on a walk that winter, she rushed her home and wrapped her in a fluffy blanket while internet shopping for dog sweaters, puffer vests, and electric dog bed warmers.

That single coat, that first little shiver, became the excuse for a whole winter wardrobe for Cat. Summer took careful measurements and ordered Cat a pink fair isle sweater, a red hooded puffer lined in faux fur, and a light blue cable knit that matched her one blue eye. That was good enough to start with. Well, no, Cat would need a raincoat as well. Yellow was classic—it would have to be yellow. That should be enough. Well, but there were those days in summer when the pavement was so hot. Cat ought to have a pair of boots to protect her paws. They might keep her feet warm in winter as well. Black. Black goes with everything. But if Cat was to have black shoes, she ought to have a black collar and leash so as not to clash. She had nearly outgrown her purple collar anyway, and the purple leash was looking dingy and frayed. Summer briefly considered some sort of hat to keep Cat's ears warm but decided that might be a little over the top. Oh well—why have a pet at all if you aren't going to spoil it? She got the hat as well—a little red knit snood with a white pompom on top like a Santa hat.

It eased Summer's mind being able to bundle Cat up warmly for their walks. Still, when the dog attempted to snuffle the dried winter grass along their route, Summer panicked that she might inhale something harmful or deadly to her respiratory system, convinced that Cat's constitution was uniquely delicate. This led to a degree of frustration in the dog, who, far from wishing to worry her companion, couldn't ignore certain urges and instincts. It particularly pained Summer to see Cat eat the crunchy dried leaves from the pavement or investigate the remains of unfortunate squirrels flattened on the roadside.

On a crisp, sunny Christmas Eve morning, Summer took a sweet fruity loaf of bread and some iced cookies to Magda, who was usually found tending her winter garden beds even on the coldest mornings. Summer placed the Christmas goodies on the little iron table by their usual bench, and Cat went straight to work snuffling about by Magda's side.

"Cat! Get out of it!"

"She's just curious, not to worry. Dogs discover their world with all their senses, but especially smell and taste. Through those delicate senses, they make sense of most things." Magda told her as Cat sniffed around the winter garden to Summer's chagrin.

"She doesn't know what's good for her. She'll poison herself."

"Oh, I doubt that."

"Have you even had a dog before? Have you had a pet at all? Besides wild birds?" Summer asked, a tad frustrated with Magda's dismissive chuckle.

"A pet? Maybe . . . oh look at that lovely loaf! Is that for me?"

"Yes! Merry Christmas! But . . . maybe? I think you'd know if you'd had a pet before." Summer said, keeping an eagle eye on Cat, who was bounding with joy into a pile of dry, crispy brown leaves and getting her red puffer vest dirty. "Don't eat them, Cat! Catherine! No leaves! Not for you! . . . Was it a dog you 'might' have had?"

"No, no. Not a dog. I found it."

"Found what?"

"Well, after a while in the desert, I had become something of a crepuscular creature. It was easiest to be active in those warm, blue hours of the waxing or waning light, at least in the summer. The sun was too strong for me to take for more than a few minutes at its apex. It still is, honestly, even after all these years. Maybe as I continue to live my life in the desert, I'll become more accustomed to it—enjoying its warmth instead of suffering its blazing fire. Of course, I know the sun itself won't change—doesn't change—but maybe I'll learn to know it better and to love it. My feeling is that I'll always have to be careful of it at its strongest, and I'll never be able to meet the sun's gaze . . ."

"You must never look at the sun, Magda. You could go blind!" Summer's eyes were round in grave concern. Magda just laughed.

"Well, meeting it eye to eye or not, maybe someday I'll feel its rays as love, like the saguaro and the chuckwalla. We experience the same thing quite differently—and I'm still an amateur among much older and wiser beings. But I still long to feel the heat as heaven and not as hell . . ." Magda trailed off.

"So . . . you kept a chuckwalla? That was your 'maybe' pet?"

"What? No, not a chuckwalla. It was around dawn one day, while I was hunting for some barrel cactus fruits. I heard a weak little cry from a broom of scrubby creosote. I don't know why, but my heart went out to it—whatever it might be. It was the lonely cry of a creature who hasn't chosen solitude but instead received it unwillingly. I'm familiar with that cry. Quite familiar. I crept over softly and discovered a tiny bobcat kitten tucked among the scratchy brush. It looked hungry. Maybe its mother was hunting and would soon return with Baby's breakfast. I found a distant vantage point downwind of the kitten and watched, just to be sure the kitten's mother came back and hadn't just abandoned him or met with some misfortune herself.

"I watched even as the first of the sun's rays slid over the horizon—its scorching fingers threatening to set my hair ablaze. I would have gone back to my cave long before then normally, but I couldn't leave without knowing that Baby was cared for. I waited and waited even as the sun crept higher and hotter. At length, someone did come—not a mother bobcat carrying a tasty dove, but a curious coyote who had heard the squawking kitten in the bush. The coyote smelled the kitten in the air and inched nearer. The kitten, silly thing, wouldn't stop its hungry ruckus or try to hide itself from the approaching danger. It just kept calling for Mother, who never came. The coyote moved in. I couldn't bear it. I just couldn't sit there and let it happen.

"I leapt up and started hollering insults at the big bully and tossed rocks at it. The coward ran off and, as the sun was relentlessly firing up the furnace of a fully broken day, I scooped up the kitten, wrapping it up in the front of my shirt like a baby kangaroo, and took him scratching and screaming back to my cave."

"My, that's quite the story, Magda!" Summer crooned indulgently with soft, condescending eyes.

"Well, that was just the beginning . . ."

"What happened after you took it home with you?"

"I didn't know what to feed it—this squawking baby. I made a thick stew of palo verde beans and mesquite meal, flavored with some prickly pear juice. It's good enough if you're hungry. I knew the kitten was starving, but he just wouldn't eat my stew.

"I toasted some barrel cactus seeds. They are lovely, fatty little things that I would save to take with me on my expeditions into the desert to forage. They were good when I was feeling especially hollow. He did eat a few of those, but they gave him diarrhea in my nice clean cave! I cleaned it up as well as possible, but it still stank!"

"Ugh! Disgusting!"

"Yes—yes, it was. I knew what had to happen. I suppose I'd always known. Baby was a carnivore. I needed to find him some meat. I thought I could teach him to survive, like me, on desert legumes, seeds, and fruit, but he kept getting weaker. I had to do something quickly, or he wouldn't make it.

"I took a bit of bungee cord from my supplies. I searched all evening for the perfect stick—forked—not too brittle. I tied on the cord and found a good stone—smooth—not too heavy. Then I waited.

"They always came because I fed them little bits of my dinner. I couldn't really spare it, but I liked their company. They soothed my loneliness, and the eventual trust they had in me was gratifying. So as usual, because of that trust, they came—their little head feathers bobbing . . .

"They came right to me because I'd taught them to trust that my hands only held a few seeds to share. But this time, I drew back the stone in the cord, bit my lip, and took my cowardly shot.

"Baby ate well that night. Soon he was purring half-asleep on my chest. He felt warm and content, trusting that I could care for him like a proper mother. But my friends, the quail, never trusted me again. Not after I robbed them of their brother or sister, parent, friend, or child with my slingshot. I didn't think it could happen . . . I wasn't ready. I never believed I could take a life with my own hands. I just wanted so badly for Baby to eat—to survive. I valued his life over theirs. After that night, I was his mother. I loved him."

"What happened to him?" Summer asked as Magda looked off toward the horizon, deep in thought.

"He grew. I couldn't believe how fast. He purred almost constantly and was always by me or on top of me. When I walked, he tried to walk between my legs. When I stood, he tried to climb me like a tree. When I sat, he was on my lap, my shoulders, or perched on top of my head. When I lay down to sleep, he would somehow take up more of my blanket than I would. I loved him. I really loved him.

"I hunted for him every day. The quail stopped coming to me, so I had to go and find them or something else. I had to try to secure the mouth of the cave so Baby couldn't get out. It wasn't easy. He could squeeze himself through the tiniest cracks, like an octopus in a maze. But I couldn't have him coming out hunting with me. He would scare off the birds—maybe even wander off and get eaten himself.

"Eventually, my stores got low. More and more of my time was spent hunting for Baby's meals rather than gathering food and finding water for myself. I wondered if Baby would ever be able to hunt for himself or if I'd always have to catch his food. But it was all right. I didn't mind it. I liked being able to feed him. Because that's what mothers do: they care for their children and provide for their needs.

"One evening, I brought him home a nice floppy branch from an ironwood tree with a couple soft feathery leaf fronds. I dragged it around the floor of the cave, made it dance for him, and he chased it around and pounced on it until the leaves all fell off, and the branch snapped in two. Then he guarded the pieces like a treasure for the next hour or so. I loved him so much.

"There were times it seemed like Baby didn't know he was a bobcat. He looked at my eyes like a real person and tried so hard to talk to me, but he didn't make bobcat noises. He sounded more like a little bird with his throaty little peeps and cheeps and chirps and squawks. I called him my little cat-bird . . . I loved him so much.

"I was almost out of dry stores. I should have been gathering more—I felt weak from rationing, and my clothes started fitting too loose. But Baby was getting plump and sleek! He started showing more and more interest—even urgency—in going outside the cave with me. But I knew it couldn't be. To let him go at that point would probably have meant his death. He'd never hunted—never had to defend himself against the wiles of coyotes. He thought the whole desert was his friend and playground!

"No, I couldn't let him out because I loved him—and he could die. It was too late for him to learn those things. He would just have to stay my baby, and I would care for him forever, though the time came when I absolutely had to go foraging for myself! Even my skin began to feel baggy!"

"I've said it before, Magda. Self-care is vital. First, you must love and care for yourself before you can care for others." Magda chuckled and looked off the other way. "Well . . . were you able to come to some equitable system for keeping both of your needs met?"

"Ask me another time. I'm not sure I have it in me tonight."

"Are you tired, Magda?"

"I am. When you're old, you feel tired most of the time—tired with the weight of memories—and all you want to do is sit quietly and watch the birds or the sunset."

"Will I see you tomorrow? Christmas?" Magda didn't answer. She was someplace far away.

1 2

Christmas

Summer hadn't willingly spent a Christmas with her parents in five years. It wasn't that she didn't love her parents—their home was merely depressing to her and seemed particularly joyless, fraught with the uncomfortable sense of both guilt and obligation. There was a scanty serving of forced jollity in the form of a shabby, synthetic door wreath and a brief exchange of practical gifts within a prescribed price range. It had usually ended with her sitting alone, listening to popular Christmas music, which communicated sentiments to which she couldn't relate, while both parents returned to work. Summer would spend most of the holiday alone in the dead quiet of an empty house. This year, she had no intention of paying to fly home for that and had been planning her own magical Christmas since August.

The day after Thanksgiving, Summer had started decorating. She bought a six-foot-tall fresh blue spruce from an obliging boy scout troop, then trimmed it one night in clear twinkle lights and all red and gold glass bulbs. She strived for the kind of sophistication and uniformity one sees in shop windows and the tall bay windows of fancy houses—nothing cheap or flimsy or fake. When she finally turned out the lights and sat by the fire with her whiskey neat to admire the finished tree, her heart was stabbed with a pang of unspeakable sadness. It was beautiful. Absolutely beautiful. But it hurt like a sad song stings an already wounded soul. She hugged Cat close and told herself it was just the lingering melancholia of past disappointments—ghosts—and focused on planning her perfect Christmas day.

The days leading up to Christmas, Summer had baked feverishly, decorating cookies to give to her neighbors, but mostly for herself. She even baked a special, odd-smelling peanut butter and chicken cookie for Cat. She had just assumed that Magda would be alone at Christmas, simply because she was always alone, except when she was with Summer. She had thought on Christmas morning of poking her head over the fence as she always did and finding Magda, as she always was, doing something or other in her garden, and summoning her over for a Christmas feast as a surprise. Summer felt good about how nice a gesture like that would be.

On Christmas Eve, after leaving Magda in her garden, Summer hung up Cat's stocking by the fire and put the odd-smelling dog cookie inside. She placed a small package under the tree for Magda, too. This would show her that Summer had planned on spending Christmas with her all along. She could barely wait to surprise Magda the next morning.

Summer knew how it was supposed to be on Christmas morning. She'd seen the movies—the excited kids—the smiling faces—the beautifully wrapped presents with sparkling ribbons and bows. When she awoke on Christmas morning, she knew she couldn't manage that kind of thrill. She'd missed it, and there was no getting it now. Still, she'd gotten herself an expensive Scotch, wrapped it up pretty, and put it under the tree to open the next morning.

When she came into the living room in her slippered feet and flannels, she went straight to her phone to start streaming some old Christmas tunes over the wireless speaker, then started a fire. Cat heaved herself up onto the couch next to her with an old-dog groan, despite her youth, and laid her chin on Summer's lap.

"Merry Christmas, Cat!" The dog cocked her head and sniffed the paw-shaped stocking Summer laid in front of her. The treat that had taken an hour to make took 15 seconds for Cat to eat, then she looked at Summer expectantly. "Sorry, that's all. Just the one. I don't want you getting a sick tummy on the rug again." The dog sighed and returned her chin to its resting place on Summer's lap. Summer then opened her Scotch and held the fancy box to her chest while watching the flames and listening to the music, but when her eyes started to mist up during *Silent Night*, she switched off the music. "Well, enough of that!" She sprang up, showered, and dressed in her most festive outfit to go and find Magda.

***

"Hello? Yes, I'd like to report a missing person . . . it's my next-door neighbor. Her name is Magda . . . No, I don't know her last name . . . Yes, I'm sure she's not at home, she's not in her garden, she's not walking in the neighborhood . . . No, no, I'm sure she's missing . . . No, I know—I know it's Christmas, but I'm sure she hasn't got family that she's gone to see. She would've mentioned it . . . She's old, senile, I think. I'm worried about her . . . The last time I saw her was last night . . . Ok . . . Ok . . . I will . . . Thank you. Please find her."

Around 10 am on Christmas morning, the local police issued a silver alert for Magda and sent out her description. About an hour after that, Summer received a call saying that the police had found her.

"Well, where was she? What? A graveyard? No, I don't know why she would be there . . . I don't even know how she would've gotten there—she hasn't got a car. Yes . . . yes . . . bring her here."

The police brought Magda to Summer's front door. Magda looked cheerful, bundled up in her brown canvas coat and customary green beanie pulled over her ears with her fuzzy silver braids draped over her shoulders.

"Summer, dear girl! You really shouldn't bother the police like that! I was out for a walk! I was going to come back!"

"Well, how was I supposed to know? You're always at home or in the neighborhood. I've never known you to leave. I was worried!"

"Well, thank you for your concern. I was just on a Christmas stroll."

"You were ten miles from here!"

"I like a long walk."

"Ten miles?"

"Why not? I'm old, but I'm not an invalid."

"That's not what I'm saying. Never mind. I just . . . you know, I was looking for you because I thought you might like to . . . well, I thought you might join me for Christmas dinner . . . and I have a present for you."

"Oh, Summer! I'd love to join you! You shouldn't get Old Magda presents, though. I don't need anything."

"Well, I just thought you might like it. It's not much . . ." Summer sheepishly handed Magda the package from under the tree. She had wrapped it neatly in shimmering paper and tied it with a red ribbon. Magda opened it carefully and held up a pair of new gardening gloves, the same shade of green as her beanie.

"These are lovely!"

"I just thought you could use them. I notice you don't usually wear gloves, and maybe you don't need them, but they might save your hands some wear and tear."

"Thank you, Summer. That was very thoughtful of you. I don't deserve it. I don't deserve you. Thank you."

Summer and Magda sat down to a simple dinner—nothing like the Christmas feasts one sees in movies—but for Summer, all things considered, it was the best Christmas she'd ever had.

13

What Happened to Baby

The new year came with a wave of anticipation and excitement. A new decade full of hope and plans: 2020. Summer swore to make these 20s roar, even as news of a virus in China started streaming in on her car radio. Still, this news was far away, and there were other things on Summer's mind since Christmas Eve when Magda had told her the strange story of a certain bobcat kitten that almost certainly never existed.

Summer didn't wish to rush her patient, but she had a feeling that whatever Magda didn't have it in her to tell that night was somehow crucial to understanding the root of her mental illness. She waited patiently and didn't bring it up again for a few days. She gave Magda some space after Christmas, avoided long conversations with her, and gave her time to feel ready to talk about it again. At least for herself, Summer knew she always had more to say when it had been a while since she could talk to someone.

Finally, Summer decided the time was right. It was a chilly January afternoon, not frigid or darkening yet. She baked up a tempting batch of chocolate chip cookies and brought a plate of them, still warm, out into the backyard. Poking her head up over the fence separating their properties, Summer saw Magda, as usual, on her hands and knees in the garden, this time wearing her green Christmas gloves.

"Hi, Magda!"

"Hello, dear Summer Sunshine! Come to brighten this chilly winter day?" Summer smiled.

"How are you doing?" Magda chuckled. She always chuckled at that question.

"Well, I'm a day closer to my death," she said with a smile—her usual answer.

"So am I, for that matter," Summer rejoined. "I baked cookies."

"Did you?"

"Yes, they're still warm. Shall I bring some over?"

"Oh yes, let's see these warm cookies!" Summer came around to Magda's front gate and lifted the latch. Magda stood to meet her, bits of dried leaf, weed, and soil clinging to her long gray braids. "Come sit under the tree, will you? Let's give those cookies a try!"

They chatted innocently about Cat, the garden, the new year and Summer's plans, and the birds. Summer used the birds as a natural segue to continue Magda's story of the bobcat kitten.

"You were going to tell me, weren't you? Whatever happened to the baby bobcat?"

"Yes, well, to tell the truth, it's still hard to talk about what happened that night, even though it was so long ago. But it's easier in the daytime, with the birds in my garden and Cat playing in the leaves." Summer half rose to make a grab at Cat's collar. "No, no, don't worry. She's enjoying herself, and she isn't hurting anything. It's good to talk about these things, but it isn't easy!"

"What happened to him?"

"What else? He got out."

"Out of the cave?"

"Yes. I don't know how. He'd gotten stronger every day—he must have forced his way out somehow. Maybe he was looking for me. Maybe he was playing, exploring, or trying to hunt.

"I heard it happen, you know . . . from a distance. It was terrifying. I knew beyond any doubt that it was him. He was hissing and screaming—the coyotes were laughing like they do. They cornered my Baby and tore his little body to pieces. I ran toward the sounds, but there were so many of them, frenzied and feasting. I had to stay back. There was nothing I could do but watch.

"I vomited what little I had in me when I saw a mother coyote feed pieces of my Baby's organs to her own babies. I can't describe it—I had stroked and tickled his soft, spotted tummy just an hour earlier. And they made a meal of it for their own squawking pups."

"How horrible for you! That sounds like a truly scarring experience, Magda!" Summer tried to be empathetic while inwardly marveling at just how much detail and emotion went into telling this bizarre delusion.

"Yes, well, life was intolerable for some time after that. At first, I was sad, but only for a short while. I wept and felt lonely and robbed, and helpless . . . again! How to describe what I felt then—I felt just massively out of control. More and more, further and further, worse and worse with each day that dawned. I felt myself careening toward disaster and the jaws of death itself! Closer every day.

"At times, I felt I was already snagged, caught in death's teeth, staring crazed down its infinite black throat. Torn between terror of the darkness and wishing with all my might that it would just swallow me and make an end. I managed to struggle back out, but each time was a more difficult and perilous climb through the gullet of death with it continually swallowing, pulling me back down into its black depths. Do you know what this is? I look in your eyes, and I feel that you must, though maybe you've never felt it so severely—so acutely—so desperately. It was anger, Summer. No, it was more than that. It was rage. And the dream! That dream!"

"What dream?" Summer sat forward, poised to catch a glimpse into Magda's wounded psyche.

"I had it most nights, but eventually, I didn't have to be sleeping to have it, which worried me. I had it sitting wide awake in the heat of the afternoon. I had it while grinding mesquite in my cave. It was always the same, or very similar:

"I would be walking at dusk in the place where they ate Baby. I would be scattering petals that floated on the wind. Then, in the deepening twilight, I would see a pair of glowing, green coyote eyes staring at me from a clump of brush. It would come toward me, hackles raised, its lips fluttering upward to show glistening teeth. I would hear its deep, rolling growl. I wouldn't run. Of course, I knew better than to run, but I felt no fear at all. I would just look at it. It would look back at me. And then, like lightning, we would fall on each other in a flash of fur and fang.

"I draw my big knife. I plunge its blade into the monster's belly, jerking upward toward its snapping jaws. All of its organs spill out on the ground, and the dying coyote drags its own entrails through the sand, howling madly in pain. It dies among the others of its pack, all of which fear me now and run frantically off a cliff to their death rather than taste my motherly wrath. And thus, Baby is avenged." Magda stopped, looking searchingly at Summer's face.

Summer could think of no response, though she sensed it was time for her to ask some leading question that might help Magda see her own dream in a healthy light. No words would come, however—just a raw feeling of *déjà vu.*

"It's horrendous. I know," Magda finally said. "I know it's horrendous and violent, and bloody, and . . . just horrendous. But in my rage, I thought to myself, wouldn't it ease this grief that's been hanging like a giant stone around my neck? Wouldn't it lighten my load just a little to have my just revenge on them for what they took from me? What they did to me? What they did to my Baby? Is it wrong to take some pleasure in how this dream makes me feel—how something dark within me applauds the scene? To take control and take revenge! To scare the scariest creatures I know with my own fearless strength and power!

"But it was just a dream. I would always wake to the ache of my empty heart in my empty cave, and I could see no way forward. There was no way forward that I could see but to find a way to take back my peace and my happiness by force—by force . . . by storm, by blood, by war on their kind— on their species! I hated them! How I hated them! The monsters! They tore my Baby's body to pieces and ate it! I hated them! I would kill them! I would kill them all! Their stinking guts would drag through the hot desert sand, and they'd know my motherly wrath! I'd make them howl for the mercy they never showed Baby. I'd make them howl and howl and suffer and die!"

Summer sat listening to Magda's highly complex and detailed delusion, shocked by the strength of the emotion, the hatred, the descriptions of violence and gore that she never would have expected from this sweet little old woman who fed the birds and peacefully tended her garden. As she listened, an odd feeling came over her—not a feeling of professional curiosity, personal disgust, or even compassion. Any of those might have fit the situation, but this feeling was different. It was that feeling of *déjà vu* again. For a moment as she listened to Magda's words, there was a glimmer, if you could call it that. Perhaps it was more of a sense or a sudden awareness of something that had settled right behind her eyes in the cavern and crevices of her skull—spanning from anterior to posterior cranial fossa, sliding over her sella turcica, and sinking into every groove, foramen, and canal: Sand.

Summer's head was full of sand. She felt like if she just tilted her head to the side, the stuff might pour out of her ear like the thin stream from an hourglass onto the ground. She had been here before. In the sand. In the heat. In the place of Magda's exile. But how? Her head was so heavy with the feeling that she held it in her hands to support it as the wave of heat hit her face.

Summer was sinking now, lower on the bench until her head was down between her knees, and the desert heat crashed over her. Not here. Not again. She squeezed her eyes shut and instantly wished she hadn't because to do so was to open the door to that place—the place she went to every time. The dry place. The hot place. Where was her lavender oil? Where were the particular words . . . the ones that helped. The ones that fastened her to reality. They had dried up and shriveled away in the heat like a plant with shallow roots. She was sinking further into the sand and couldn't move her limbs, except slowly, awkwardly. Magda had spoken to her, but the sand was in her ears and in her mouth as well. Her words were slow and slurred.

Summer struggled mentally to swim out of the hot sand. Fear gripped her that it might cover her over completely this time and spill into her lungs. What if she couldn't breathe? What if her heart stopped beating? What if she died here? She looked down at her clothing. As before—as always— as in all the times she'd been there before and nearly died, she was dressed in a scratchy white dress with velcro up the back and rough lace around the collar: a doll's satin wedding dress. She wanted to scream, but no sound would come. She wanted to tear off the horrible doll's dress. She wanted to come out of that place. It had been so long since she'd been there. It had been so long since she'd felt the hot sand choking her and filling her head, burning her cheeks . . . burning . . . burning . . . *freezing*!

Cold! Cold! Cold! What was it? Summer's body reacted instinctively, recoiling, springing up. Her eyelids peeled themselves back, and there was Magda, spraying her with the garden hose, relentlessly soaking her and the plate of cookies next to her, there in the cold January garden.

"Stop! Stop! Please!" Summer shouted, holding her hands out in front of her face to block the torrent.

"Are you back?"

"I'm here, I'm here! Just stop! Please!" Magda put down the hose, cranked the tap shut, and handed Summer a rough towel.

"Talk to me," Magda said. "If you don't, you might slip back." Summer didn't know what to say. She knew Magda was right, but she struggled to find any words.

"I don't know what to . . ."

"Tell me a joke."

"A joke . . ." Summer faltered.

"Here, I'll tell you one first. What did the right eye say to the left eye?"

"What?"

"Between you and me . . . something smells." Summer chuckled feebly at Magda's joke. "Your turn."

"Knock knock." Summer murmured.

"Who's there."

"Little old lady."

"Little old lady who?"

"I didn't know you could yodel, Magda!" Even though the joke was old and worn out, they both laughed, and Summer started to feel more firmly as though she were back in Magda's garden and that Magda's garden was reality.

"What did the mother fish say to its baby at bedtime?" Magda asked.

"What?"

"I blub you."

"Okay, okay . . . I don't think we need any more jokes," Summer groaned.

"I'm sorry."

"No, don't be. It was helpful."

"No, I'm sorry I took you there. If I'd known you were so close, I would have been more careful."

"What are you talking about?"

"The desert, Summer! The desert!"

"But . . . how . . ."

"I didn't know you were so close to the sandpits, or I would have been more sensitive in my telling. Do you remember how long you've been here, my dear?"

"I don't know what you're talking about . . . I just had a panic attack. I've had them before, but no one has ever sprayed me with a hose while I'm having one . . . especially in the middle of winter!"

"Well, you were struggling a little too much for my liking. A little struggle is good for you, but you were pretty deep in it. I thought it might be best to cut your session short. You need a cup of tea."

"You say the strangest things, Magda, but thank you. It worked, and thank you for not calling 9-1-1."

"Why would I have done that? They can't do anything."

"Well, my parents did once, and I ended up spending four hours in the hospital, having a CT scan and a stroke assessment. Waste of money."

"Stroke? What nonsense!"

"Well, I don't blame them. It scared them. But I know how to handle a panic attack now."

" . . . clearly," Magda said with a sidelong glance. "Shame about the cookies, though," she said, examining the little piles of mush on the plate.

Summer went back to her own house that evening, got into dry pajamas, and sat down with her notebook and a cup of herbal tea by the fire:

Had a panic attack this evening while Magda was telling more details of her desert delusion. She has had terrible dreams—very violent and angry. Not sure what triggered my attack. Magda sprayed me with the hose and told me jokes. She is so strange, but it helped. She said I have been in exile as well. Her delusion obviously assigns universality to her own perceived experience. Interesting.

14

Mother of Wild Beasts

Summer awoke the next morning feeling lousy, fragile, and a touch embarrassed. As she drank her coffee wrapped in a fuzzy blanket on the screen porch, she saw Magda's green beanie pop over the fence next door, followed by her crinkly eyes and sparse smile.

"How are you feeling this morning, Summer Dear?"

"I'm fine. Thank you for your help yesterday . . . with the hose, I mean. I'm much better now . . . in fact, I'd like to hear what came of your dream—the one you had so many times. Do you still have it now?"

"Oh, Summer . . . are you sure you want to hear about it? I don't want to hurt you . . ."

"It won't hurt me. I had an un-triggered panic attack. It happens sometimes. I have strategies for getting through them. But never mind me. Tell me more about your dream and how it made you feel." It made Summer feel better about herself to focus on Magda's problems, and she came out to the fence in her slippers. Magda crossed her arms over the top of the fence and rested her chin on top of them.

"Well, the dream was just the start. Have you ever been offered the gift of a dream come true, Summer?"

"No, I don't think so. Sounds nice, though," she said, taking a sip of steaming coffee.

"Well, I have, and I hope from now on to have more peaceful dreams because it is truly fearsome to live out a nightmare—to watch it unfold before wakeful eyes on solid ground in the heat and sweat of a living moment."

"Good grief—what happened?"

"I was walking one evening, just like in the dream, by the site of Baby's murder. I came across a beautiful flower. I'd never seen one so beautiful, and I didn't know its name. I plucked it and started to pull off its petals, scattering them on the warm breeze. Then, just like in the dream, I saw them, the green eyes peering out at me from a bush. It started toward me, and since I knew how the story was supposed to go—I'd seen it a thousand times, after all—I went forward to meet it.

"It leapt up toward my face, the coyote, and I grabbed the folds of skin around its neck roughly in my hands. Coyotes are not as big as all that. In my dream, it was bigger—more like a wolf than this scrawny, gangly little dog-thing. This one was still young. Not some pack's alpha male—the battle-tried, battle-scarred leader and paterfamilias. It must have been less than a year old. Still a pup, in fact. Gripping its neck, I threw it to the ground on its back and sat on it.

"It was an absurd scene, I'm sure, had anyone other than those cackling cactus wrens been there to see. I sat there, just gripping its snapping face between my fists full of skin and fur. I had to figure out a way to get to my knife since both of my hands were busy keeping its teeth from finding their target. I growled from the depths of my rage and shouted and cried and glared into its green eyes, shaking it. Just shaking it. Pounding its head down against the ground. It stopped struggling. It stopped snapping. I thought I might have my chance to reach for my knife at last, but then I heard it: a faint whispery, whistle of a whine. It came from deep in its throat, and then it licked me. It licked my wrist. It looked at me out of the corner of its eye, offering me a clear shot at its jugular, as they do to show their submission. It just lay there—showing me its neck, its belly, its vulnerable parts—and it cried.

"I understood what was happening. It was saying that I had won. I had unwittingly used its own language—the language of the pack, and it was offering me its obedience . . . and its trust in my mercy. Mercy! But I didn't want to show mercy! They hadn't shown mercy! Why should I? But it cried, and it licked, and it showed me its soft parts, just trusting me! I didn't know what was worse—that I was behaving so thoroughly like a coyote, or that at that moment, even with its cry for mercy and its trust that I would actually give it, I thought to myself: *I've got you now, you worthless piece of filth! Now you die!*

"But a thought requires consent to become action, you know. I had a choice in that dread eternal moment. To follow through and take my revenge according to my deepest desire and the dreadful dream that I was now living out . . . or to let the poor thing go and go myself to contemplate how it could be that I had become so much like a coyote myself that the thing had understood me so completely.

"Yes, I had a choice, then and always. In every moment, I have a choice, and I am *not* a slave! I am not a tiny bubble tossed on the sea. I'm a person! I'm a person who can say yes, and I'm a person who can say no. And I did. I said no that day. I let it go. It stood up slowly, cowering, looking at me askance, and then it trotted off with its tail tucked low. I returned to my cave that day with my own tail tucked lower still in shame.

"Oh, the fear! The terror! Still, to this day, it is appalling to think that I've allowed myself to indulge in such rage and such dreams! That I've actually spoken the coyote's vernacular and dominated him like a puppy! The relief, too . . . relief in the knowledge that one can say no. That having said it once, it may be said again and again if need be. That in the end, we are not our thoughts! And we are not our dreams! I am not my thoughts, and neither are you! We can turn them away. We can refuse them, ignore them, laugh at them, and see them for what they are!

"Oh my dear girl, how angry we've been! That's what took you there, isn't it? The memory of anger that never really went away. Anger that's covered over in the heaps of sand and the passage of time—hidden but still there. Still fresh, just covered over with other things—distractions. Well, on that day, I learned that I must make peace with the desert and all its creatures if I was to survive. I had to make peace with the birds, whom I betrayed, with the wild mother whose baby I took and spoiled, and with the coyotes whom I despised and plotted against in my heart, though I'm no different from them.

"I was alone again after that day. Not even the quail came near me. To them, I was no different from the coyotes who murdered their babies to feed their own. It may be the brutal law of wild things in the desert, but it is not the law of love. I decided on that day that I would never kill again. Never. It's startling to realize how close I was that day long ago. I held another life in my hands and wanted to destroy it in my grief. Yet even before that, I held other lives in my hands—lives that trusted me, and I justified their theft with the excuse that Baby must eat. I couldn't have believed myself capable of bloodshed before. I know myself better now . . . losing Baby was a severe mercy."

"A severe mercy? What do you mean by that?"

"It hurt, Summer. It hurt to lose him. But we were doing each other no good. In fact, I was hurting him, holding him back from the life he was meant to live. And for me, he had only ever been a grand distraction."

"From what?"

"From loneliness? No, maybe not that. Maybe a necessary alone-ness is better."

"But Magda, that's what pets are for. Every pet is a distraction from loneliness. Someone to care for, play with . . . even fuss over a bit." Summer said, stroking one of Cat's silky ears as she sat next to her by the fence, leaning against her leg in her pink fair isle sweater.

"Cat was rescued—the unfortunate product of overpopulation and irresponsible human behavior. But I should never have taken him—made him my baby and my creature—dependent forever on my care when he could have taken care of himself. I sentenced him to death the moment I took him from that creosote bush.

"I had been sitting smug in my exile and didn't even realize it—thinking how splendid I was to have nothing and want nothing. And yet, I failed this one simple test: To love something without wanting to possess it, making it utterly mine. I didn't just surround myself with stuff; I took a life—and I stole so many more just to keep that one fed. No, I was in exile without being detached and spent my time like everyone else, just grasping for more and more and more distractions and things to fill the emptiness. But I'm worse, you see. Most people only grasp at things. I've grasped at lives."

"Oh, Magda!" Summer exclaimed. Why was this kind old woman so very hard on herself for something that probably never even happened? What a dreadful place her mind must be!

"In short, dear girl, I failed. I failed to admire the flower without picking it—and thus killing it. I picked a flower and stuck it in a glass of water to make me feel less lonely—to make me feel needed and maternal again. But flowers can't live in a glass. It only preserves them for a moment, then they die. And as for feeling maternal? Real mothers teach their babies how to live without them. I was no mother. I was a slave owner. I am still ashamed. It still hurts like the sun at midday."

"Magda, this guilt is doing you no good! You need to move on. You are one of the kindest, most generous people I've ever known, and I hate to hear you talk this way about yourself!"

"How little you know me, Summer. It's like the books, you know? Like the books, and the garden, and pets, and family. It's always something.

Always. There is always something or someone to pour myself into—whether obsession over Baby, obsession over the coyotes and taking revenge on them, or obsession over that ridiculous desert novel I tried to write years ago that nobody would ever read. And these were only ever to distract me from thinking about Maxim and Blaise. But, then again, thinking about them was to distract me from the horrible panic of nothing to think about at all! You see how many layers to this there are? If I have distractions to distract me from my original distractions—what do the original distractions distract from? More distractions?"

"I don't—"

"We have to become archaeologists, Summer! We have to chisel away, slowly, painstakingly, at all the strata of distractions that are crushing us! It's hard, patient work, cracking through the ancient, hardened layers that we have allowed to bury us alive. For myself, I finally remove one layer only to find another, harder and thicker than the one previous. Oh, that brief moment of excitement—believing that I'm finally uncovering soft, vulnerable, Precambrian consciousness only to find I'm still on the Phanerozoic surface, sifting through heaped-up rubbish and dung."

"What do you think you'll find? At the end of all your digging?" Summer was uncomfortable with Magda's use of the pronoun "we."

"I'm afraid, Summer. I'm afraid that the creature I finally discover, assuming I discover her at all, will be very small and weak and stunted—translucent from its life of darkness—slight and malnourished. She needs sunlight and real love, not this obsession and need—this lust for possession. She is, that is to say, she must be, the seed! The seed of what I am meant to become—some flowering bush or fruit tree if I can reach that degree of health . . .

"But, I grow so old, so very, very old—I feel now how close I am to death. I'm heavy and precariously balanced. It's as if I never noticed that my humanity was being buried long ago, in some deep, inaccessible tomb at the center of my soul. Retrieving it has been the purpose of my exile, this whole painful journey. If I am to find peace at last, to hear the song of the stars and encounter its promise, I must keep chipping—keep digging—mark the site of my realization of these truths with a few stones piled one on top of another, and move on from it, always forward. And this realization, though the cruelest the desert has given me even to this day, is still better than continuing on in ignorance."

"Oh, Magda! You aren't ignorant! You're so concerned about doing what's right, you should be more gentle with yourself! How can you be expected to love anyone properly when you can't even love yourself?"

"I can't love myself when I know what I have been. I saw myself as a good mother—a caretaker, a guide, and perhaps to the greatest extent, a protector. I called it motherly wrath before. But I've been utterly possessed by The Mother of Wild Beasts—consumed in anger and made a beast myself by it. And once that strong wine of wrath was tasted, I drank it nearly to the dregs. Nearly. I came so close to taking that life with my own hands, purely out of revenge. What puff of fresh air cleared my vision at the last minute? What ray of light broke through the storm clouds? It feels as though someone has been very gentle and gracious to me in my illness."

15

The Dream

What a dreadful place Magda's mind must be! So tortured, guilt-ridden . . . full of such hideous imaginings and violent scenes! The interpretation of dreams and delusions was not an area of expertise for Summer and seemed to her a flimsy, pseudoscientific pursuit anyway. Still, she felt there must be some trauma at the root of these inventions. They were told with such pain, such feeling, that Summer often found herself sucked into the story as though it were real. She continued to find herself transported to the very desert Magda described, as though she were reading a book—a hard but very good book—the sort so entirely immersive that it feels more real than reality.

What Summer couldn't quite wrap her head around was why the feelings of *déjà vu* kept creeping in at those moments. And why Magda claimed so insistently that Summer was there with her—that she had been there in Magda's desert for most of her life. It must be part of the delusion—a delusion of universality, of shared experience. But that didn't change the bizarre yet unshakable feeling that she really had been there and that in the midst of her most profound moments of panic, a desert was where she went.

Was Magda describing some state of mind in poetic terms? Perhaps, but why such effort? Why such artifice? Why the attention to detail with these desert scenes painted fantastically in words? Why couldn't she just say what she meant in simple, everyday terms?

Summer recorded every conversation now, secretly, on her mobile device, innocently placed on the table looking idle. She transcribed them faithfully every night and pondered over the strange old woman's account of her "exile," wondering, testing, reading, trying to solve the problem that was Magda. There on her red couch, Summer would describe every non-verbal detail, every expression and gesture. She would organize, categorize, ever striving to identify the underlying pathology she knew must be present.

Summer was consumed with an overpowering, missional urge to de-code the Magda Enigma, and having solved it, make her well again. She stared into the dying embers that evening as they languished and breathed their last in her fireplace. Cat groaned, stretched out her back legs, then snuggled up to Summer with a contented sigh. Nothing was more reward-ing than being faced with a problem yet having the absolute conviction that it could be solved and resolved. It only needed thinking.

That night after Magda described her experience wrestling with the coyote, Summer stayed up late, playing and replaying the story recorded on her phone, trying to figure out if something in it had triggered her panic attack. The story's intensity was shocking, to hear little old Magda with her crinkly eyes, missing teeth, long silver braids, and shabby green beanie de-scribing such a blazing, blinding rage. It was unbelievable, and yet there had been times—long ago—after Catherine—times in the tree, times in her room with the door locked—times with her pillow wrapped around her face as she felt the moist heat of her own muted screams—times when she wanted to break something—anything—just crush it in her hands as if it would ease the constant crushing of her own heart—a crushing that never seemed to end.

One learns impulse control, of course. One learns to sublimate, count to three, or ten, or fifty, take the breaths, take the beat, have those secret and subtle rituals, and eventually behave like the grownups do. One learns to be reasonable, sensible, logical, and above all, responsible for one's own actions and reactions to unpleasant feelings. Some things are best tucked away. Other people's pain was much more accessible, diagnosable, fixable. Her own could be ignored, most of the time.

These uncomfortable memories floated in and out of Summer's con-sciousness to the recording of Magda's voice, telling over and over again how she wrestled the coyote. Summer's eyelids felt sandy. Was she tired, or was it left over from her panic attack? She closed them to ease the scratchiness, just for a moment as she listened to Magda's words in the recording. *I've been utterly possessed,* her old voice wavered again and again. *Possessed . . . possessed . . .* Summer yawned . . . *I've been utterly possessed . . . possessed . . . I've tasted the strong wine . . . tasted . . .* Summer's breathing deepened and roared like a desert wind in her own ears . . . *I've been utterly possessed . . . utterly . . . tasted . . . I've utterly tasted . . . I've been . . . I've tasted . . . I've been consumed* . . . Summer's body went rigid. She began sweating, her heart knocked against her chest . . . *I've been consumed . . . by . . . possessed by . . . tasted the strong wine . . . nearly. Nearly. I've been utterly possessed by the Mother of Wild Beasts—made a beast myself by it.*

Nearly.

Summer was sinking into the searing hot sand. She was in the scratchy white doll's dress again—her body powerless to move. She wanted to scream, but her voice was silent; not even a faint rasping wisp of a whisper could be forced from her lips. Her chest was tight. The sand was all around her and up to her neck. It was in her ears now, and her nose and eyes. She couldn't move. She couldn't scream. She couldn't breathe. And yet, she couldn't die. She couldn't stop.

Suddenly, she heard a faint whistling through the sand's roar, hot in her ears. A whistled tune then hummed—a woman's voice, strong and ringing from the deepest place in a woman's chest. Then she felt it, a hand grasping hers and pulling hard, singing now: Magda's song.

Magda's song flowed on and on, shimmering, blending, sliding, merging within itself, its iridescence suggesting colors both familiar and shockingly new. Summer felt herself breathing again. Felt her rigid body releasing, her chest loosening its grip around her thumping heart. She could see it now—she could see the song, its colors shimmering in the hot desert air like the distortions of the solar wind in an aurora. She was lying atop the sand, and the deep ringing voice sang on. Summer watched the song arch through the sky in sliding purples, greens, and blues—feeling it distantly as both a warmth and a light. There was a depth to the song that frightened her if she looked long enough—not because of its content, which didn't make any more sense now than it had before, but because of its familiarity.

It was as if she were catching glimpses of a place she had been when she was very young—the kind of memory so early yet so trenchant that it only exists as a confusion of colors and feelings. She felt as though it might come into sharper relief if she focused on it long enough. But when she really concentrated on it, the colors receded, and it was like looking through the wrong end of a telescope—just a pinpoint of colored light at the end of a thick blackness—blues and greens and golds—a severe light, but beautiful. No, it was seen best without trying—without analysis and study, which seemed to make it hide itself from her.

There was a goodness about the song—an innocence. It had a cooling effect and seemed to wash the sand out of Summer's head and ears. She had lain long listening and watching the song when the strong hand pulled her to her feet and started walking. *Where are we going, Magda?* Summer asked wordlessly, voicelessly, in a thought language that she felt sure would be understood by this singing apparition. It sang on, stronger and more insistently, pointing toward a horizon shifting and shimmering with rising heat. *What's out there?* Summer asked. The voice made no answer, but Summer felt certain that what was out there, where the sand met the sky, was no different from where she stood. There was nothing. No difference. No well. No oasis. No sea. *I don't want to go there, Magda. It's no different over there, and it's too hard to get there.*

The song stopped. The colors faded. A hollow silence surrounded them like the gray stone walls of an ancient chapel might absorb the notes of the cherubic hymn as it ends, leaving only its memory and a feeling. *It isn't different. But you will be if you make the journey.*

I don't want to be here anymore. I want to leave the desert and never come back.

You can't, dear girl. You can't leave the desert.

But why? Summer felt her eyes brimming with tears she couldn't afford to shed in that dry wasteland.

Because the desert isn't a place at all . . . it isn't some remote geographical region you can choose to visit and leave whenever you wish. The desert is within you . . . you can't escape from yourself. It will follow you wherever you go. It will follow you into the forest, the ocean, or the mountains. But you still must make the journey. You must find a well.

What if there isn't a well? What if there's nothing? Just more sand . . . more pain. Magda . . . what if there's nothing there at all? The apparition grinned and chuckled, as though Summer had suggested something absurd. The strong hand that had pulled her out of the sand pulled her forward, though her feet were heavy and hot. It felt to Summer as though her muscles had no strength to move, and her greatest efforts resulted only in the smallest movements. *I can't move . . . I'm just so heavy . . . and tired.*

Just keep trying—I'll stay with you for now. Hold my hand, dear girl. We'll go together for a while.

Don't leave me.

I'm not leaving you yet.

Don't leave me at all! I'll die! I'll sink! Just let me rest someplace safe for a while! The apparition laughed again.

Baby, you can't stay in the cave. You won't learn how to live! Stay with me for now, I'll teach you how . . . but I can't do it for you. Summer clung to the apparition's cool hand like a frightened child. It seemed as though they trudged and labored through the deep sand for many years . . . decades . . . centuries . . . before a sound woke Summer with a jerk. A scratching, scrabbling noise on the back patio. She peered through a gap in the blinds to see a 'possum dragging away her bird feeder while Cat watched silently.

"Some guard dog you are, Cat. And where were you when I was sinking? You could have woken me." She scratched behind the dog's soft ears, noticing that her shirt was drenched in sweat, cold, and clinging to her back. She must have panicked in her sleep. That hadn't happened in over a year. Perhaps it was time for that pill again—the one that made her mind go blank. The one that made her sleep without dreams.

Summer washed her face in cool water, changed into clean pajamas, and breathed deep the lavender oil she'd dabbed on her wrists. She looked at the orange medicine bottle in her cabinet. The anti-anxiety medication she saved for the worst of times. She wavered, then shut the cabinet.

"I shouldn't have fallen asleep on the couch."

16

Pandemic

February arrived, and with it news of infection. Cases of that far-away virus were beginning to appear in other places—closer places. Medical face masks and hand sanitizer started to disappear from store shelves. The next month brought an insanity Summer could never have believed possible. Cases in the next county over. Cases in the city. Hospitals full. Classes canceled—postponed—moved to online platforms—shelter in place orders—empty grocery store shelves and toilet paper shortages. She rushed along with everyone else, faces shrouded in bandanas, balaclavas, and other makeshift masks—through the long lines, the carts full of canned beans and dry pasta—bottles of bleach and cases of wine and beer to weather the quarantine.

The world was going mad with fear and anger. Anger over what? Anything. Everything. And politics as usual. Summer gathered what she could—dry rice and beans, flour and yeast, tubs and tubs of old-fashioned oats, dog food and chocolate and coffee—and planned to stay inside her house for as long as it would take for the virus to be brought under control, for a vaccine to be developed and distributed, and for the world to return to its senses.

Only Magda seemed unbothered—unchanged. Summer informed her of all the news and the advisories. Still, Magda's comings and goings never altered. Except for her one long walk on Christmas day, her movements were utterly predictable. It occurred to Summer that Magda would probably need some supplies. At her age, she shouldn't be entering into the throng and lines of people. Summer gathered up some of her own supplies in a box and took them over to her one morning. The spring weather was beginning to warm Magda's garden, and she was out hand-tilling her vegetable beds in preparation for planting. Summer hefted the box onto the garden table.

"Magda, it's crazy out there. You shouldn't make trips out unless you absolutely have to."

"Oh, I don't need anything anyway," Magda shrugged.

"Well, this could go on for quite some time. It might even get worse! I've brought you some supplies, just to help you, you know . . . so you don't have to go out for anything. It's nothing fancy. Rice, beans, oats—and I even managed to find some toilet paper!" Magda just laughed.

"Are you frightened, Summer? You seem troubled."

"Not for myself . . ." Summer faltered.

"Why then?"

"People like you, Magda. Older folks are dying from this. I just want you to be safe. You will listen to me, won't you? You will be careful?"

"It doesn't affect me. I've been in quarantine for over forty years! I'm in practice for social distancing." Summer laughed. It was a relief to know Magda was so isolated. The very thing that had concerned her for months about Magda's lifestyle was a blessing in time of pandemic.

As spring unfolded and the death toll climbed, things returned to what had come to constitute normality in Summer's interviews with Magda under the apple tree. Summer had little else to do with herself, and so she came to hear Magda's stories every day while she helped pull weeds in the garden.

Magda had learned when to stop. She observed Summer closely now when she told stories of her exile, watching for signs that Summer was slipping. Magda took her only so far. As soon as Summer's cheeks began to turn pink and her head began to drop with the hot sand's weight, she pulled back and said something absurd. Magda was good at absurdities and always had several at the ready to pull Summer back into the moment on the garden bench under the apple tree. Summer was aware of this shift in Magda's storytelling technique. She was impressed. Magda was more astute than she had given her credit.

But it still irked Summer beyond reason that she kept slipping at all. It must be the stress of those extraordinary times. Or was it? When Magda spoke, she caught glimpses again of that hard place—dry and sharp—the sea of searing, choking sand—as though her mind contained a high stone wall, and Magda's words came to her from the other side of a crack in that wall. Perhaps the wall was there, and perhaps it wasn't. Perhaps it was just a creative way to think about something else quite scientific and well established. But then, perhaps it was precisely what it seemed to be, and she had built it herself, brick by brick, to keep the sand from seeping through into her safe, clean space—her productive and practical space—her lavender-scented, grown-up, ambitious, and happy space.

Summer felt the presence of that wall as surely as she felt the presence of the vastness beyond it. It worried her. She wanted to focus on it but couldn't quite bring herself to it. Perhaps she feared what fossilized remains and memories she might dig out of those shifting sands, or perhaps she feared most of all, finding nothing at all in the sand but pain. Pain upon pain, and no safe return to the protective shelter she'd worked so hard to build. She could always shift her focus to the news. The protests. The politicians. The drama of a world in chaos proved surprisingly less stressful—a serviceable distraction even, from what lay beyond that wall.

As Summer stared into the mauve clouds one evening as spring was transitioning to summer, listening to Magda's voice slipping quietly into that iridescent soap bubble song, it occurred to her that Cat had been very quiet. Perhaps too quiet. Looking around the garden rows, now thick with kale and spinach leaves, Summer caught sight of Cat's head bobbing up and down behind the broccoli bed.

"Cat!" Summer shouted. The dog's head shot up at the sound of her name. Her snout was caked in soil. Little dark clumps clutched and clung to her eyelashes and whiskers. Magda's young broccoli plants lay in partial ruin. Summer sighed and pulled Cat by the collar toward her own yard, and the dog, digging in her heels, slid reluctantly through the gate.

"That was naughty! You don't do that again," she said, then wearily proceeded to pick up what might be salvaged of Magda's baby broccoli plants. She worked silently, with her forehead knit in abstract thought that flowed between past and present. It felt as she ran her fingers in the cold, moist soil, as though she were raking up her own memories, trying to salvage something she'd hoped for, planned for . . . but which had been viciously torn up before her eyes and lost forever.

"Catherine," Magda said. She stood watching Summer gouging her now blackened fingers through the soil, trying hopelessly to replant Magda's torn up leaves. Summer stopped, looking up at Magda in shock and fear. Her hands trembled.

"You're thinking of Catherine, aren't you?" Summer stared down again at the torn-up vegetable patch. The moist soil formed cold, dark wet patches on her knees. Finally, she exhaled, running soiled fingers through her hair and meeting Magda's patient gaze.

"I don't know why. I don't know why I can't forget her, or at least stop thinking about her—stop hurting over her. I guess I just wanted her so badly."

"She was your sister, wasn't she?"

"Yes. Yes, she was. I saw her, you know. They let me hold her. She was wrapped up in a blanket—warm and pink and perfect, but tiny . . . just far too tiny . . . and she didn't stay warm for long."

"I know," Magda said, and she really seemed to.

"Everything was too small. She was just so early, you know. My dad asked me to find one of my doll's dresses for her. Was that fair? I don't know . . . I just don't know. I remember looking at my dolls and all their dresses, looking for one that was small enough . . . but pretty, you know? I wanted her to have something pretty. In the end, I picked out my special porcelain doll's wedding gown. I remember taking it off of her, ripping open the velcro down the back. It was scratchy. The lace was scratchy too, but it was pretty. Everything else was just too bright. Too pink. Even at that age, I had some idea that she should have something appropriate for a funeral."

"How old were you?"

"I was seven."

"So young."

"I wanted her to wear something sort of solemn. Serious. Because she looked serious. Her face was so serious. Peaceful, pretty, and pink . . . but serious. I picked the wedding dress because it was just white. Like an angel or something."

"Yes, I know."

"By the time I saw it on her, she wasn't pink and pretty anymore. She was gray. She looked like a cold little lump of clay in my doll's wedding dress. Why did they leave that little white casket open? Why did I have to see her like that? Did it make them feel better? Did they think it would help me? It just scared me! And for so long after that day, I couldn't look at my porcelain doll. I hid her away, her naked cloth body missing its dress. One night I finally broke her. I smashed her porcelain face . . . that happy painted smile . . . I bashed it in on a rock in the backyard. I thought it might help me forget if she wasn't there anymore, smiling at me without her dress. Maybe it did help a little bit. But Catherine's cold little gray face peeping out from that scratchy white dress that wasn't hers never went away."

Summer didn't weep. The words came like rain from the sky, but her eyes were dry. Magda never said a word. She sat on the soil silently next to Summer, holding her hand and stroking it gently. She didn't ask leading or probing questions as Summer would have done in that situation. But the gentle love and peace she radiated pulled words out of Summer that she had never told anyone else before.

"I wanted a sister so badly . . . but I knew I couldn't ask again. My parents . . . my mom especially . . . they were different after that. Quiet. Sad. Their eyes were red, and there were nights my mom never slept. She just cried in the rocking chair. My dad would come and hold her hand and never say a word. Then, finally, they stopped crying. They went completely dry—dry and flat. They were just numb, and dry, and flattened out . . . like paper cut-out parents.

"How could I have hurt them by asking them to risk so much pain again for me? Because *I* was lonely. Because *I* wanted it more than anything in the world and would have given anything and everything for a sister—or a brother—I didn't even care which anymore. Just someone. Someone to share my childhood, my thoughts, my room, my love with—to share my secrets, and hold my hand. I knew I couldn't be that selfish. I saw their pain, even when they went flat and dry. It never went away. Mine didn't either, though sometimes it seemed like anger. Sometimes it seemed like fear. Often it seemed like hunger. Yes . . . hunger most often. I was so very, very hungry. I took secret food to my room, and I ate . . . but I never felt full. Never."

Summer paused, looking at the now customary plate of baked goods they had been sharing. This time it was pumpkin bread made from some of the canned pumpkin Magda gave her in the fall. She felt the urge to take a piece but didn't.

"Time doesn't make it better," Summer said. "It just makes you bigger and sweeps you along. You just react. You deal with what comes as it comes, and that's what I did. I did the things other people were doing because I didn't want to stay there and be sad with them. I didn't want to be home anymore. I didn't want to see them or be like them. I went to college. I made plans that scared them . . . that scared me, but I did them anyway. I was still so very, very lonely, though . . .

"It is morbid," Summer admitted. "I realize it's morbid, naming my dog after Catherine. But I *saved* her, you see? She would have died. They would have euthanized her because there are so many dogs and so few people willing to take them. I could save her. I did save her. I was helpless back then . . . helpless to save my sister, but I saved a puppy for her and named it after her . . .

"Oh! I'm sick!" Summer clutched her stomach. "I'm in so much pain, Magda! I thought it might help, but it makes me sadder, and Cat! I can't discipline her firmly because of who she is. She's the one I saved, and I love her. I love her so much, and she will die! A dog's life is so short, and I can't bring myself to scold her when I know how much it will hurt when she's gone too."

Summer's eyes finally spilled over with the years' worth of tears she had swallowed. Still, Magda didn't speak but reached her arm around Summer's shoulders and held her close as she convulsed with tears that she felt might drown her; so many had been held back for so long. She looked up to see Magda's eyes cascading tears as well and felt her own ease up, as though Magda had taken hers and was crying them for her. Finally, they sat simply and quietly, watching the dusk close in through the apple tree's budding branches and the humble, honest song of the spring breeze sighing in its limbs.

"You need to make a trip, my dear."

"I can't. No one should be flying right now."

"You can drive."

"I don't want to."

"Needs must be prioritized over wants. Anyway, your summer vacation is coming up soon. You need to go. You need to go and visit your parents. You need to hold them, hug them, talk with them, heal with them. You are all they have in this world. They need your love, and you need theirs."

"I've given them enough. I gave them the silence they needed when I felt like screaming. I gave them space when I needed closeness. It's my turn now. I have to take care of myself! The greatest lesson I've learned in my life so far is that I must love myself first. Care for myself first."

"It doesn't work like that. I think you know it doesn't, but you've heard it said so many times that it seems like it must be true."

"It is true! I mean it!"

"Of course you mean it. And it may even be half-true, or a quarter-true, but you are so young—you say things more than you mean them from the sheer force and exhilaration of meaning something at all. No. No, Summer, the more you care for you and only you, the more it will hurt. Care for them. Love them. Forgive them. Comfort them. That's what will heal you. Go. Plan your trip, and don't wait. You can use the time on the road to think. Make your peace and give them everything you wish you could have for yourself. Trust me, Summer. I'll care for your Catherine while you're away—just go."

17

Cactus Dream

She walked across the scorching sand, her bare feet burning, her stomach churning, her soul yearning. "I'm afraid. Afraid of everything. I'm afraid of death. I'm afraid of disappearing, of being forgotten and unimportant." She said this to the tallest Saguaro—the one with the uplifted arms—the quiet witness. "Why do I feel this way? Like everything is coming to an end so fast before it has properly begun, and everything I do now has to be awesome, and earth-shattering and blow their minds?"

"Who?" asked the Saguaro. She hadn't expected a response. She had never received one before.

"Who?" it asked again.

"The others—you know."

"Who?" it asked, as if it didn't know.

"Them! The ones to whom I'm already dead! The ones who buried me while I was still kicking and screaming! The ones who wouldn't let me in—wouldn't look at me, hear me, hold me. The ones who wouldn't let me talk—wouldn't let me scream. The ones who were so knowing and thought I was so simple. How could I possibly have anything to say? Anything worth hearing? The ones who were so sad and thought my sadness less important than theirs." She traced a gentle finger down one of the Saguaro's smooth pleats. "I hate that I care—it's over and done. Still, it feels as though it never ends—it happens again—every time I remember her . . . remember them."

"Who?" said the Saguaro, as if it didn't know.

"You know—them."

"Who?" the Saguaro insisted.

"Them! The ones I don't want to be. The ones I never was . . . the ones I can't have been."

"Who?" the Saguaro pursued.

"The cold—the stoic—the distracted—the ones whose feelings mattered more than mine . . . I tried so hard to bring them back to life by being what they wanted . . . but all I was, in the end, was me."

"Who?" asked the Saguaro.

"Me! You know," she said, looking up at its stubbled face, outlined against the dusky sky.

"Who?" the Saguaro insisted.

"I don't know . . ." she whispered with a sense of horror, "I've often wondered. I don't know what I am exactly, but it wasn't what they wanted . . . needed. It wasn't what I wanted either. I was the one who didn't know what to say. Didn't know how to react, how to laugh, how to move on. I was only good with those who couldn't help."

"Who?" asked the Saguaro.

"Oh, you know them, I'm sure," she said, searching the Saguaro's ancient face.

"Who?" the Saguaro insisted.

"The wild ones. The children, of course. I was good with the children, or at least I thought I was. That's why I'm here. That's why I'm doing all of this . . . I don't want them to hurt like . . ."

"Who?" said the Saguaro.

"You remember. You were there. You've always been there."

"Who?" the Saguaro insisted.

"The one I was. The one who was crushed and angry and bleeding inside. The one I've struggled and still struggle to escape. The one I'm trying to kill so others might live. The one I almost killed one night, when I was drunk on wrath . . . I didn't, but I wanted to. It was wrong of me. I don't deserve to be happy. They aren't."

"Who?" asked the Saguaro.

"Everyone!" she cried. "Everyone—everyone I've ever known, except maybe one. I'm sure I'll never be anything like I ought to be, anything like her. I'm stuck in the past. Afraid of the future. Afraid much more of the present moment . . . but that's where she lives."

"Who?" asked the Saguaro.

"You know who."

"Who?"

"The one who pretends to be insane."

"Who?"

"The one who knows more than she says."

"Who?"

"The one who sings."

"Who?"

"The one who lives here but doesn't seem to mind it."

"Who?

"The one who tells me to get up and look for a well . . . to try again. I don't want to try again, and fail again, to be content with my loneliness. To be okay with what's happened. To embrace the tiny, frail, emaciated creature who clings too tightly to all the wrong things. I'm tired of the desert. I'm so thirsty."

The dusk was glowing behind its soft feathers, ruffled by the breeze, when the early owl took flight from the Saguaro's arms, raised as if in benediction.

"What should I do?" she asked the Saguaro, staring with trust at its wise old face, but the cactus was silent. The cactus was silent, and the owl was gone.

"I know," she said, turning slowly away. "I know I must press on." She turned and saw that toothless grin, more beautifully radiant than the russet tones of sunset—a withered hand pointed to a pile of stones. Together they knelt down and piled them, one on top of another—a cairn of stones at the site—the place they were leaving behind. Then Magda took Summer's hand in hers, a grip belying the appearance of frailty. They left that place together, and the rest of the night, Summer slept more deeply than she had for many years.

18

On the Road

On the first morning of her summer break, Summer started driving. This 2,800-mile road trip would wreak havoc on the annual mileage allotment for her leased vehicle. Still, this was an important trip. She knew it was, and even though it would mean over 40 hours of driving time round trip, she knew it was probably safer than flying, even though flights were relatively cheap. She'd heard stories, heard the news, and she wasn't going to take any unnecessary risks. She would sleep in her car when she felt too tired to drive and avoid staying in any hotels of dubious cleanliness.

Summer started driving early that morning, a thermos of coffee in the cupholder, a bag of granola bars, mixed nuts, and chewing gum on the seat next to her. The sky was pink at sunrise, and Summer started shuffling through the music on her phone, looking for the appropriate soundtrack for this sudden and momentous journey.

An undergraduate elective course in music appreciation had convinced Summer a few years back that the popular and country music she had grown up hearing on the radio would no longer fit her aspirations. Her new life would be lived out to the backdrop of classical music.

Summer started her journey with a baroque mix, hammered out with nearly robotic precision by Glenn Gould. Now, this was how life ought to be, she was convinced—clean and conventional—played with absolute control and intention—the separateness and clarity of every note—a perfectly organized contrapuntal masterpiece executed with proficiency and dispassion. How the structure of Bach's fugues and partitas calmed and reassured her that there was order in the universe! Order, pattern, and perfectly timed polyphony executed with faultless accuracy were evidence of a well-arranged and healthy mind, she thought. She knew nothing of Glenn Gould personally, but he ranked high in her estimation after hearing his recording of Bach's Goldberg Variations. Such a shame that someone could be heard groaning in the background, but she still admired the recording for Gould's virtuosity at the piano.

Around Memphis, Summer thought about turning back. She was already tired of driving, and the rain had been coming down constantly since Birmingham. Six hours. Six hours and she'd eaten all her granola bars. There were still the nuts, but she didn't really want them. She had only packed them because it seemed like a mature choice. It was lunchtime, so she went to a fast-food drive-through just off the interstate. She hated herself for not finding something more sophisticated but, having fortified herself with a burger and fries that her tastebuds thoroughly appreciated, she determined to keep driving.

Having resolved to keep moving west, Summer shifted her musical mix to Dvořák—his New World Symphony and Slavonic dances. It seemed like appropriate music for a road trip across the wide-open spaces of America. Although she admired the orchestral color and texture, it didn't represent the life she wanted for herself. It was probably more like what she had, though—soft and raging, peaceful and frenzied, melodic and chaotic—a confusion of mixed and shifting emotion that swelled and receded like a tide, sweeping her along with it. Chaos is beautiful when it is someone else's, and Dvořák's chaos was some of the most impressive in her opinion, but it is difficult to love one's own. She could admire Dvořák's emotional preoccupations, just as she could enjoy hearing about other people's problems, but she didn't want them for herself.

When Summer pulled into Oklahoma City, dusk was falling. She had left the lush forests of the Southeast behind, and a morose, brooding mood overtook her. She didn't want to be here. It was starting to feel more like what she had left behind, and she felt an old familiar heaviness returning. She kept driving. Her credit card was defrauded at a gas station in Amarillo. Thankfully she still had her debit card to use. She slept for a few hours in Tucumcari, where she was lulled into irrational, absurd dreams by Stravinsky's Rite of Spring, which she tried ever so hard to like, but never quite could.

Joaquin Rodrigo's Concierto Aranjuez brought Summer into Albuquerque early that morning, with evocations of its history as an 18th-century outpost of Santa Fe de Nuevo México, a provincial kingdom of the Spanish Empire. She purposefully drove through the old town plaza, mostly deserted at that early, blue-gray hour. She parked and walked by the old San Felipe church, one of the city's oldest surviving buildings. She had never seen it when she was growing up. She had never seen much of anything of cultural significance there or in Santa Fe. Now, standing in front of the impressive old church just touched by the golden light of the rising sun, she felt a pang of regret that she'd never realized how beautiful her hometown was after all.

Summer stopped for a breakfast burrito with extra green chile from Twisters, one of the few things she freely admitted to having missed about home. She walked with it down into the cottonwood bosque and ate by the river, watching the brown waters drift by while a scrawny coyote on the other side watched her. Then, having fully saturated herself with piñon coffee, another thing she might have missed just a little bit, she knocked on the door of the little brown stucco house where she had spent her childhood.

Part II

1

Taken

Summer leaned forward onto the steering wheel as she finally entered Atlanta city limits that August. She couldn't get home fast enough. She stared intently in the direction she imagined her little house to be. She might have been disoriented. In Albuquerque, she always knew where she was because of the Sandia Mountains east of the city. Here, it was hard to figure out cardinal directions because everything looked the same to her. Everything was overgrown with kudzu and surrounded by trees—but she felt a tug, perhaps like a pigeon in the direction of its homing.

It dawned upon her in an instant—a feeling she hadn't anticipated. Without even realizing it had happened, Summer had made herself a life, a home, even her own odd little family. There was love waiting for her in the wagging of Cat's whole back end and in that ridiculous buckshot grin that Magda gave her over the fence. It moved her almost to tears. She was no longer alone, and she was almost home.

Summer ended up spending most of her summer holiday with her parents in Albuquerque. Once she was there, it was hard to imagine getting back in the car and driving all that distance again. Anyway, the time spent with her parents ended up being cathartic.

Summer had followed Magda's advice and simply loved her parents. She showed up on their doorstep that morning in June, smiling, though she was sure that it looked forced because it was. She hugged them both, holding them longer and tighter than she felt was typical upon such meetings. She baked bread for them, serving it warm with canned peaches she had brought with her from Magda's garden. She cooked meals for them—meals from scratch made with real butter and fancy cheeses and herbs. When her parents returned home from work, they would all sit and enjoy her kitchen creations together.

Summer told her parents about her new life in Atlanta—her dog named Cat, her cozy fireplace, and her friend next door. She slept poorly in her own room—for what grown-up finds sleep easy in a haunted house? Still, she made up for it with naps snatched here and there in her father's easy chair.

How many times had she told them that she loved them—missed them—appreciated them—thought of them? She said it every day that summer and hugged them every morning and every evening. They smiled. It had been so long since she had seen them smile. They seemed bewildered as if they sensed some secret behind her presence and her words, but they didn't question it. They simply accepted it and returned it as much as they were able.

She asked them questions about when they were young, about when they first met, about their own parents, their grandparents. She told them she was sorry for being away for so long, and she almost, very nearly, sort of actually meant it. She promised to call home more often—to text them sometimes—to love them better. They cried. She hadn't seen those poor dried out people cry since she was a little girl mourning the loss of a premature baby sister. They held her close. They said things—not all the things she'd wanted to hear—but they said they loved her, and her heart felt a little warmer. Maybe that was all she needed, after all.

She smiled, and it wasn't forced anymore. She cried, and it wasn't sad or shameful or immature. Summer finally left them and started driving the long road back to her home in the Deep South, but it didn't feel quite as far anymore. In fact, they felt a great deal closer than they ever had, even when she was still living under their roof. And now she was going home.

Summer returned to her house that soupy evening in August to a deathly quiet. She turned on the lights, cranked up the air conditioner, unpacked her things, and made a cup of tea. It felt marvelous to be out of the car! She had been sitting comfortably, happily on the red sofa for only a minute or two when she began to wonder. Surely Magda had seen her arrive—she saw everything. Why hadn't she come over? Where was Cat? There was no sound of her eager barking, which always signaled that she had caught Summer's scent. She looked through the window toward

Magda's house and saw no light coming from inside. She had never seen Magda's house dark before. Something was terribly, terribly wrong.

Summer sprang up from the sofa and ran outside. She banged her fists on Magda's front door. There was no sound within. She peered over the fence into the garden, but there was no sign of her familiar form bent over the vegetable beds—no sound of her singing her song—no Cat rushing to the fence with her tongue lolling and backside wagging. Summer circled around to the other side of the house where she met Mrs. Turnipseed taking out her garbage.

"Are you looking for Crazy Magda?" she called over to Summer.

"Yes, Magda . . . do you know where she is?" Summer hadn't realized until that day just how much she disliked Magda's neighborhood nickname.

"No, I don't know where she is exactly, but I know something bad happened a few days ago," Mrs. Turnipseed said in a dramatic, gossipy sort of way.

"What? What happened?" Summer walked over to Mrs. Turnipseed, who quickly reached into her pocket, pulled out a flower-printed fabric mask, and covered her nose and mouth. Summer took a step back, remembering to keep six feet of distance between them.

"It's those new people. You know, the ones who moved in just recently, on the corner—or maybe you weren't here when they moved in. You've been away, haven't you?"

"I just got back. What happened?"

"Well, Magda was doing her rocks, you know how she does. Their kids were out in the yard playing, and the mom called the cops on her. Said she was dangerous to the kids, dangerous to the neighborhood, disrespectful of people's property. Said if they didn't come and do something, she would take matters into her own hands. Went on about her rights to protect her own property and family. She wrote up a doozy of a rant on the neighborhood forum later."

"Oh, no! Did they come? The police?"

"Oh, they came. Took them a while, apparently. You could hear her up the street yelling at them for taking so long. Said Crazy Magda could have stoned her children dead in that amount of time."

"Good grief! What did they do?"

"Took her away. Not sure where. Animal control came and got the dog out of the garden the next day. She was making a racket—howling, whining. I'm thinking our new neighbors called that in as well. Haven't seen either of them since."

Summer didn't bother to wait another minute, even to be polite. She ran home and started making phone calls. It was easier to find Cat than it was to find Magda since the dog was microchipped. The next morning, she went directly to claim her from the animal shelter, took her home, and fed her before leaving again to search for Magda. It was no easy task finding her when she didn't even know Magda's last name. The police wouldn't tell her any details of Magda's arrest or where she'd been taken. With the help of one of her psychiatry instructors who had colleagues in high places, Summer finally located Magda at a state-run nursing facility.

"I'm here for Magda." Summer said to the administrator.

"Are you family?"

"Not officially."

"Well then, officially, I'll have to deny your request."

It took a painfully long time. Magda had no living relatives that anyone could discover. Eventually, after a lot of red tape and official paperwork, Summer was named a legal guardian with power of attorney, and Magda was released to her care. She could finally take her home.

2

Maxim and Blaise

It was evening when Summer finally got Magda released. The late cicadas were ringing in the warm, heavy air as she brought Magda inside her own home. Summer quickly lit the candles in the fireplace out of habit and put the kettle on for tea.

"Oh, what a pretty little fire!" Magda edged timidly toward the three small flames. "It's so alive—so small, but it really fills the room, doesn't it?"

"Come sit, Magda. Watch the candles all you like. I'll make us some tea."

"Tea! Oh, that would be a treat!" Magda sat herself down in the crook of the red sofa's arm, and Cat curled up next to her, resting her chin on Magda's lap. Magda stroked Cat's ears as she watched the flickering flames, a faint smile on her lips.

"I'm sorry about what happened, Magda," Summer called from the kitchen. She got out two new matching mugs she'd purchased from a gallery in Albuquerque's Old Town. Magda didn't seem to hear. "Magda? Magda, I'm sorry about what happened while I was gone. About the neighbors reporting you . . ."

"What did you say about the neighbors?" Magda finally tore her eyes away from the dancing flames.

"I'm sorry about what they did—calling the police on you like that! Such negativity and drama! It was totally uncalled for."

"Oh, that. It doesn't matter."

"What do you mean? Of course it matters!"

"I mean that I don't do what I do to get their approval or their thanks. I'll still do it . . . maybe at a different time of day, though—when the children aren't out playing. I think they thought I was aiming at them."

"You're not going to stop? Magda! They don't like it! Most of the neighbors don't care because they know you aren't doing any harm. They make allowances because you pull their weeds and give them pickles. These people don't want you near their house . . . at all!"

"I'm not hurting their house."

"They think you are."

"They just don't understand. I'll do it when they aren't around."

"Magda, everyone is always around these days, and no one understands . . . I don't understand!"

"It's okay. You don't have to understand. I'm taking care of it. Listen to Old Magda, Summer. It's for the best."

"No! Magda, you listen to me! I got you released to my guardianship and supervision, and I am telling you—you can't be upsetting people anymore by throwing rocks at their houses. I'm ultimately the one responsible now!"

"But what about . . ." Magda rose from the couch in alarm.

"What?"

"Well, someone has to keep them away—this street is absolutely infested!"

"Infested with what?" Magda paused and sat back down, looking at the candles again.

"I don't want to frighten you, Summer."

"I'm sure you won't."

"I'm the only one who can see them, apparently, so I'm the only one who can chase them off. Anyway, they wouldn't listen to you, even if you tried."

"And why do 'they' listen to you?"

"Because I'm Old Magda! I've been here long enough; I know them all by name! I don't engage with them personally, but I know them, and they certainly know me."

"What is it exactly that you know about them?"

"I know enough. I know they don't belong. I know they don't mean well. And I know my responsibility. I don't chase them away to get anyone's thanks or good opinion, and I don't care if you all think I'm insane. They don't belong here. Let me help."

"Name them, Magda. What are you chasing away?"

"No. I won't. Not until you've seen them yourself. Then we can talk about them. For now, it doesn't do you any good to have a name for something you don't believe is there."

"It's not there. There's nothing there. Whatever you think is there, it's not. I want to help you. I want to keep you—keep you in your house, keep you out of trouble. You're my friend, Magda. The closest thing to family I have right now. You and Cat—you're all I've got! Please! I . . . I need you. I need you to stay out of trouble." Magda's face grew grave as she took in a deep breath.

"We *are* family now, aren't we," she said. "The desert brings people together. You never find quite what you want, but you find what you need, and that's better."

"What did you want to find?"

"A way back—a way forward—a way to be with Maxim and Blaise. Anything but stillness. But the stillness was what I needed . . . stillness and you. I'm not sure why or how, but you're going to help me, Summer. Probably not in a way either of us expects."

"I *am* going to help you if you'll let me. Please just trust my judgment." Summer brought the two mugs of tea to the coffee table and set them on coasters.

"Did it help you to go to your parents? Did you see them for who they are? Did you love them?"

"I loved them. It was good . . . not what I wanted. But, like you said, probably what I needed." Magda smiled and sipped her tea, turning again to the candles. "But don't think I've forgotten," Summer added.

"What's that?" Magda said knowingly.

"You said you would tell me about Maxim and Blaise when I told you about Catherine. Well, you know about Catherine now . . ."

"Yes, I did say that, didn't I."

"I'm listening. We have tea, some cozy candles . . . now tell me about Maxim and Blaise." Magda smiled and cleared her throat.

"Let me see, it was the summer when we moved into the new house. We'd lived in an apartment downtown when I was younger. My father worked in a factory. When his mother died, she left him with a little money she'd saved up, and he moved us to a house with more space in and around it. The first time I saw Maxim, he was playing in his front yard, across the road from ours, with a little red wagon. He was putting rocks in it and taking the rocks to the back yard where he was trying to build a stone fortress, the kind you might find as a remnant of medieval Europe, with slit windows for firing arrows at intruders."

"How old were you?"

"Seven . . . maybe eight. I was in the flower bed, collecting roly-polies—you know, those little gray pill bugs. I was putting them in a little bucket. I remember the plinking noise they made when I dropped them in."

"You were neighbors, then?"

"Yes."

"Did he come and ask you to play with him?"

"No. I yelled to him across the road and asked if he would like to buy one of my roly-polies. He said he didn't have any money. I said I would take a piece of candy or gum instead, but he didn't have those either. I asked him if he would just like to play with them with me, and he said no to that as well. He said he was awfully busy. I found this intriguing since it was usually only grown-ups who were busy and serious, so I thought he must be extremely mature. I asked what he was so busy doing, and he told me he was building this wall—this stone fortress—and had to keep collecting rocks for it."

"And he asked you to help him?"

"No, I just did it. There was something about his task . . . something about him, that made me want to stay and help. We didn't speak much, except about the relative merits of different rocks that we found and how they could best be used. We found many good rocks by the little creek that ran through the fringe of trees behind his house. We worked all afternoon. Children used to be able to do these things, you know. Play outside all day without much interference. Perhaps it sounds strange to you now. We collected all the rocks we could and then began to build this curving wall, and Maxim was very clever about such things—structures, designs."

"How big did it get?"

"Oh, quite tall. Maxim had gotten a step stool from his father's workshop to reach the top level of stones, and I pasted them with mud from the creek that I'd collected in my bucket for mortar. We placed a few sticks and branches as buttresses for extra support. It was around suppertime when his mother came out looking for him and found us, little Max and Maggie, in this magnificent structure—a hideout of stone and mud and sticks. At least *we* thought it was magnificent. We felt very proud, making plans for the next day's additions when his mother came. We thought she would be impressed with our work."

"Was she?"

"Maybe. But she told us we mustn't build stone walls and fortresses anymore and to carefully dismantle that one. I remember her words so clearly."

"What did she say?"

"She said, 'this is no fit playhouse for you two. It could easily crush you if it fell.' We hadn't thought about that. We had never imagined that it *could* fall, let alone on top of us. I remember staring at our fort, unable to quite believe that this beautiful thing our hands had built could hurt us. Then I heard my mother's call—she mimicked the white-throated sparrow's call when she wanted me—and away I ran to her sheltering wings."

"So that fort was knocked down?"

"Yes, Maxim and his father dismantled it that night. After that, his father helped him build a treehouse, and he and I read books in it during the summers that followed. It was a good, sturdy treehouse that lasted many seasons with careful upkeep, but we never forgot our stone fortress. He told me that someday when we were grown-ups, we could build it again. *Really* build it. I suppose we did . . . but his mother was wise, after all . . ."

"Did you marry Maxim?" Magda smiled.

"Yes. I was 23 when we married, just graduated from the women's college. He was so handsome—tall, with kind blue eyes—and he really was kind. That was one of the first things I loved about him. A truly kind soul. Kind and serious. We were happy. We built the house, you know. My house. He built it; I just had ideas, but he built it with his hands."

"That's amazing."

"Yes. Yes, he was amazing. And Blaise . . . sweet Blaise! He came along later—a beautiful boy with eyes just like Maxim's. He was so tiny and soft. His hair was like feathers. I had both of them for a short but wonderful time."

"What happened to them?"

"It was Christmas Eve. Maxim took Blaise with him to get a Christmas tree. I was home baking Christmas cookies. It was wet, starting to be icy . . . no one wore seat belts back in those days even if your car had them. No one had car seats for small children . . ."

" . . . and you were spared."

"No. *They* were spared. I was left behind." Magda took another sip of her tea and sighed as she watched the three little flames. "Blaise was five years old. I was pregnant with his sister. I lost her that night after I got home from the hospital. I lost them, then I lost her, and I woke up Christmas morning in the desert, no tears left to shed . . . just a terrible headache. I wrapped my tiny baby girl in my prettiest scarf and planted her in the garden. You know the cairn of stones in the corner . . . that's where."

"Oh Magda . . . I'm so sorry."

"And that was the beginning of my exile."

"So it's true, then. The desert wasn't real . . . your exile. You were never really in the desert. It wasn't real . . . just a metaphor." Summer had always told herself that Magda's story was a fantasy. Still, something about hearing the facts of Magda's life made her mourn the last possibility that maybe this strange old woman had actually lived alone in a scorching, howling desert, foraging for food, sleeping in a cave, and searching for a well. Something about her story and its telling had been so compelling, so real! Summer felt her heart sink as she heard the words that she had long suspected—that Magda was just another casualty, like herself, of loss. But Magda grabbed Summer's hand and squeezed.

"Of course it was real! It *is* real! I'm still in it, and you're in it with me! You know it's true! It may not be factual, by scientific standards, but it's true! We can avert our minds from it, distract our dried-up hearts with overcast dreams, but no dream can last, or bring real relief. It's a mirage. That's all it is. We can't escape the desert; we just have to learn its lessons. We have to find a well! We have to help each other. I was alone for so long, but now I have you! I lost them in the dead of winter, but now I have received the gift of a sweet, beautiful Summer!"

Summer smiled as she started to understand. To Magda, the "desert" had always been a state of heart—a state of soul—simultaneously grief and hope: a bright sorrow. It was never a delusion—the product of an unquiet mind. It was a poeticized narrative, and Magda truly was a tragic genius.

The two desert-dwellers stayed up until midnight when a soft rain began to fall to the rumble of distant thunder. Their parched souls were sprinkled with a gentle rain that slowly sank in and soothed them both. Then Magda hugged Summer and went back to the house that Maxim built.

3

The Unattended Moment

Life went back to a normal of sorts—or at least closer to normal than the earlier part of that year. Schools were planning their reopenings with new rules and regulations for face coverings, distance, and sanitation. Summer resumed her evening visits to Magda's garden, only now the desert stories meant something different, something deeper and more profound. They weren't merely delusions to unravel, and Magda wasn't a patient to diagnose. She was a fellow traveler through the strange, dark, desert lands of shared grief—a grief Summer had ignored and done her best to cover over with hopes, dreams, ambitions, and baked goods. Now Magda's case file had become a diary—a strange personal narrative where Magda's exile and Summer's merged.

There was just beginning to be that touch of fall in the quality of light one evening when they sat quietly, saying nothing. Summer had stopped asking so many questions. It wasn't that she no longer had any, but an awed respect had dawned upon her in the past weeks, which prevented her from seeking more and more stories for the satisfaction of her own curiosity. The stories came when Magda was ready to tell them, and as time passed, it was Time itself that loomed large in her mind and words.

"It sometimes feels as though this moment—the isolated instant in which I become more aware—is some ragged shard. A piece of something that broke a long time ago, and I've let myself forget. I see its shape sometimes, this fragment, and I'm reminded of what it came from—the pattern of the whole—if it were to be somehow reassembled like a puzzle. And it *is* a pattern full of motifs and refrains. I wonder . . ."

"Hm?" Summer murmured, gazing upward at the leaves of the apple tree, illumined by the evening sun.

"Maybe it has all been just one moment lived over and over—one song on repeat—the same chance given time after time at the bridge—to discover that every moment has been an annunciation—a dangling question, waiting for my answer. It may be that a lifetime is a mere moment in the scope of Time and the universe, but I believe that a whole lifetime can blaze in every human moment if we can bear to be present long enough—every moment spent blazing is from gazing at the Sun. Perhaps that's why we keep looking away. We can't bear it long. But once we look away, somehow we forget—forget everything—forget that dangling question—that invitation."

"Sometimes I wish I could forget . . ."

"We mustn't forget! And how could we? When you are in the moment, it seems absurd to think you could ever be the same again once you're out of it. I come full circle in the song. I come again to the chorus—the ultimate meaning of the song. It's an invitation, and I know it because I've heard it so many times. How can I have forgotten that I've been invited, not to observe from a safe distance, but to participate? I've been invited to a dance. Will I, won't I—will I, won't I—will I join the dance?" Summer smiled.

"I know that one."

"I've really gone down the rabbit hole now, haven't I?" Magda grinned briefly, but her face went sober again. "And just like that, the bubble is burst. I don't know how or why, but I'm out of the blaze now. Reeling. Everything is dark and blue, as it is when you walk indoors after a long time lying in the sun. I think I would prefer to be completely burnt up by dancing and sun gazing in a Wonderland that I can't begin to understand or explain than this distressing back and forth motion. The unattended moment may be less painful, Summer, but it's also less beautiful. It is simply surviving. It is an invented place to shelter from the truth and the fear of healing."

"Fear of healing?" Summer frowned in thought.

"Well, healing would be a betrayal, wouldn't it? Can I be allowed to laugh again? Can I be allowed to find a flower or a bird beautiful and dear? Can I enjoy the sweetness of a peach or enjoy the laughter of children, the smell of baking cookies, or the glow of Christmas lights on a winter's evening? I can allow distraction if it makes life bearable, but I can't accept a cure. For being cured would mean I didn't love them. Being cured would mean forgetting, and that can never be."

"That's not really how you feel, is it. I know what you're doing, Magda. You're telling me how you think I feel and trying to make me feel better about it by speaking in the first person. I know that trick." Magda smiled.

"And yet . . . and yet . . . Summer think of those moments in the Sun! Our eyes and hearts scorched by the purity of its rays! When you're in it, can't you almost believe that there is a Love beyond these loves? A healing beyond forgetting?"

The two of them returned to silence—a silence that was no longer uncomfortable—a silence that bore greater significance than any spoken word could have held. It was a moment on repeat, as Magda had said—their moment in the garden, under the tree, in their desert, but each repeated chorus, like a spiral staircase, took them just a little higher than the last.

4

Two Paths Converge

Summer awoke the next morning in a fog, though the sky was clear and bright. She had gone away last night, somewhere beautiful she could no longer see in her mind's eye, but she felt its lingering sweetness and tried hard to remember where she'd been. She wanted to go back. She knew something important last night, and now she'd forgotten it again. Why couldn't she remember? It seemed simple enough when she was half-asleep, not trying to remember it, but all she could do in waking was to chase it around in circles, like Cat chasing her own tail. How could something so close and deep feel so far away once the day had broken?

"Magda, I think I had a dream. Not a bad one," Summer said, leaning over the fence that morning. "I've been just wandering around the house thinking and not thinking—trying to catch it again. Thinking and not thinking. Does that make sense?"

"Of course, Summer."

"It's craziness to care so much . . . isn't it?"

"I wouldn't say that, but they do call me Crazy Magda," she chuckled with a wink.

"I hate that name. They don't know what they're talking about."

"Hardly anyone does. But what is it you're caring so much about, dear? You can tell me in the abstract—that's often all I can manage."

"Thank you, Magda . . . I know I can feel safe telling you. With you, I can care about things like this and not care because I don't think you probably care if I care or not . . . right?"

"I'm not exactly sure how to answer that. I care to understand what it is you're caring so much or so little about."

"Oh, you know! Being impressive! If only I could have cared and not cared back when I was making all these choices for my life. If only I could have detached myself from caring . . . detached, right? Detached from the expectations and valuations of them . . . of everyone else!"

"Oh, I see what you mean. Yes, that must be the first to go. Caring about how everyone else sees you. You can't be too sensitive. When you're the only sane person in a room, everyone else is bound to think you're mad."

"I don't want to go back, Magda. I don't want to be swept back up into this pretense of proper and normative cares . . . caring to fit in—caring to be praised—caring to look the part—caring to seem successful and professional—caring to be seen to advantage, respected, and admired . . . I want to be okay with being . . ."

"Yes?"

". . . small."

"Ah. You don't want to go back to school this fall."

"I don't know. I'm tired of pretending. I just want to stay with you in your garden and figure things out. I don't want to care anymore, about all that at least. I want to care about what I've neglected to care about and stop caring about the rest. I want an exile like yours, Magda. An exile that leads somewhere. As it is, it feels like I'm on a treadmill, running faster and faster only to stay in the same place. I want to lose my mind and find my soul!"

"John Muir, about the forest. A nice sentiment, but exile isn't romantic, you know."

"Romance! I don't care about that. I want silence and to heal, like you. The fact is that there is no hope of an unpublicized life where I'm from—my generation. There is no quiet place. There's only constant feeding and gorging on personal details—we're full to bursting with it— and yet, still so empty! I can't do it! I can't hold on to what I find here and still go back every day to that place . . . to that way of life. Could you live out your exile in the constant presence of others? I think the answer is obvious, isn't it? Look at you! Look how you have spent your exile. Facing it! Choosing it! Again and again, you choose it, no matter how it looks to the people around you! I will lose everything I've found, Magda! I'll never catch that thought that eludes me every morning if every morning I'm met with more and louder invitations to distract myself from the fact that I've forgotten something that's a matter of life and death! I need silence!"

"It's not always silent." Magda said quietly, looking down at her hands.

"I know—I've disturbed your quiet."

"You're fine. That's not what I mean."

"What do you mean?"

"You can't expect it to be a silent, romantic exile full of beautiful, comfortable healing, free from distractions or disturbances. There may be more to distress you if you go this way. There are monsters, Summer. There are voices. The more distractions you shed, the more they will come for you."

Those voices again. Magda hadn't mentioned them in months, and Summer had nearly forgotten about them.

"Won't you tell me about the voices?"

"What can I tell you? How can I show you . . . in the quiet you go on thinking your natural thoughts, the ones that mean something and the ones that are just jibberish, but sometimes there are answers. Sometimes it's not just you answering yourself. One day long ago, I thought to myself that I needed to gather some food and find some water. Just a simple need, a practical and straightforward thought, but that day there was an answer:

"But there won't be anything
and you'll probably die soon,"
a soft, appealing voice lamented
and it really seemed to know.

                                     "No, we must try to find
                                  good food and water. Don't
                                  lose hope in finding a well,"
                             another soft voice interjected.

"Hope is gone. You might as
well be dead," said the first voice.

                                    "Don't say such ridiculous
                                  things! There's always hope!"

"You were a terrible
mother—a terrible wife!

You've brought this on
yourself, you know."
That first voice was relentless.

I'm not! I'm an excellent mother! Probably better than most! And I'm a
terrific wife! Or at least I used to be! I yelled at no one.

"Let's not go too far.
You had your faults,
but you did your best."
The softer voice said.

"It's your fault, all of this!
Your failure put you here!"
The first voice said.

I did my best! I loved them! I loved them so much! I cried inwardly.

"And now they're dead.
They needed you, but you
weren't there to save them."

"Don't listen to that nonsense.
It's not your fault—none of it."

I know it's not . . .

"But isn't it, really?
Shouldn't you have
been there with them?"

Maybe . . . maybe if I'd been there, I'd be with them now instead of
here . . .

"It's not worth thinking
these things. You have to
stay calm and focus on

finding a well."

"You'll never make it in time.
You'll die here all alone."

I have to try!

"You *will* die if you don't start
moving in the right direction."

"There might be some water
in the wash over there in the
distance. It's a little greener."

"That's far out of your
way, though. It's a well
you want, not a mud hole.
Anyway, you really can't
afford to take detours."

I do have a little water left . . .

"It's not enough. You're going
to die out here. Even if it is a
mud hole, there's no promise of
anything better anywhere else."

"Of course there is! There's a well!
You should go now! There's no more
time to lose debating its existence!"

That second voice really did seem to know . . . *I should. I should go that*
way. I should go now . . .

"Stop! You don't know what
lies that way! Use your eyes!"

"Go! There's no time to lose!
You have to start moving! You
don't need to see! Have faith!"

"Oh! Stop it! Stop it! Be quiet!" I screamed aloud into the silent desert. Perhaps I knew it was the wisest thing to just make a start and trust that the well was out there if I walked in the right direction. Yes, I did know. But that frantic voice kept shouting my deepest fears—appealing to my practical nature, blaming me for everything—that I had been selfish—that I had failed them. I took a small sip of my remaining water and started walking, not toward the green area that may or may not be water . . . in the direction that I knew the well must be. I walked and walked while the voices continued their bickering in my mind.

"You should've gone to the wash."

"Quiet! You lost that round!
I know what you're trying
to do, and I won't have it!"

"You have no power here.
You're *long* gone."

What are you? What am I to you? Don't you have anything better to do than torment me? I spoke silently in my mind to the bickering voices.

"Don't mind us."

"Don't mind *him*.
Just keep walking."

"No, you should absolutely stop!"

"You absolutely *mustn't* stop!"

"You'll run out of water—
you'll overheat—you'll die!"

"Stop trying to scare her!"

I'm not sure I can keep going. I don't have it in me . . .

"Good! Stop! Go back to the wash."

"You can do it! Don't go back!"

I'm so tired! But I won't go back. No, I won't go back.

"You know, on second thought,
maybe you should run! You'll
get there much faster if you do!"

"Running will only exhaust
you. Just keep on walking!"

"You could at least walk a little faster.
You'll never get there at this rate."

Maybe I could walk a little faster . . .

"Don't push too hard. You need
to rest under that ironwood tree.
Pick a few seeds to sustain you.
then get up and keep walking."

"Don't rest! Go faster!
How could you be so selfish!
Think of Blaise!"

I won't rest.

"Rest!"

"Don't rest!"

I won't!

I walked on, jogging intermittently. The midday sun beat down on me so that it felt like I was going slowly up in flames. Still, the voices argued. Still, I refused to rest. Still, my water supply dwindled, and the few remaining seeds in my pouch grew fewer.

"You're going about this all wrong, you know. Trying to take it by force— stubbornly refusing to pace yourself. You'll kill yourself getting there. Where's the love in that? Smells more like pride."

"It has to be this way!
Face it head-on! Don't think
so much about yourself.
Honestly, could you be any
more selfish? Just try harder!"

I'm trying!

"Take a rest. Be still. Listen."

"Don't slow down!
You rest—you die!"

"That's not true. You won't meet Him like this anyway."

Who? Maxim?

"Yes, Maxim!"

"No, not Maxim."

"Don't bring Him into it."

Who?

"Don't ask!"

                                              "Yes! Ask!

Who?

"Blaise!"

                                              "No, not Blaise."

"Blaise is everything."

                                              "Let go of Blaise."

Let go of Blaise? What does that even mean?

"It means nothing."

                                              "It means everything!"

What then? Just tell me what it means!

                                              "Remember Baby?"

"Don't think about Baby.
It's too painful."

                                              "Lean into the pain.
                                              Let it transform you!"

It hurts.

"So don't do it!"

                                              "Lean! Keep leaning!

Think about Baby."

I can't!

"Then don't! If it's
hurting you don't . . .
but go faster! Faster!"

"Don't go faster!
Think!
Think about Baby!
You have to think
about Baby!"

What does Baby have to do with Blaise?

"Nothing!"

"Everything!"

Stop it!

"You stop! Now!"

"Don't stop!
Go, go, go!
Faster!"

Maybe just a short rest . . .

"No!"

"Yes!"

Yes, I will . . . just for a few minutes to catch my breath . . . but I won't think about Baby!

I made for a scrubby ironwood tree and carefully swept the perimeter for snakes and scorpions (visible enemies are easy enough to find) before sitting under it in the little scrap of shade it offered. *Please, please just stop talking.* I said to the incessant nobodies. As it seemed to me, they talked and talked but never really said anything—at least nothing that made any sense. The one said things I wanted to hear but didn't entirely trust. The other spoke pain I didn't want to dwell on, but I knew was true.

I leaned my head against the trunk of the tree, and for a time, there was perfect silence. No words. No suggestions. No accusations. No demands. I sighed and took a tiny sip of water. I shut my eyes for just a moment. It felt wonderful to close them.

But the darkness behind my shuttered lids couldn't last. Only too soon, there was a face filling my mind. A whiskered face with yellow eyes. Baby. *No, please, not him!* In my mind, I watched myself caring for the kitten, carefully sequestering him in my safe cave. I watched him devour the creatures I killed for him to eat.

Why didn't I take him with me? Let him out to learn how to do things for himself . . . remain true to my quail friends?

I imagined a different scene—a better one. I imagined myself taking Baby out of the cave to let him practice hunting. I saw him grow bigger, stronger, and more independent. I waited patiently as he began to spend more of his time alone in the desert until one day, he didn't come back. Somehow, I knew that he would be fine. His time had come to leave.

That's how it should've been, I thought.

> "Yes, but you wanted
> him to need you.
> You muddled love
> and need until they
> were the same thing."

I loved him.

> "You did, at first.
> But the love you
> had for him became
> unwholesome."

How can a mother's love be unwholesome? It's the purest love there is!

> "Your love became a
> lustful, possessive

outpouring of your
own selfishness.
Your need to
be needed."

I'm sorry! Tears I couldn't spare rolled down my dusty cheeks. *I'm so sorry! I just wanted someone to care for again! Like I used to care for Blaise when he was tiny . . .*

"You were given a gift
more precious than the
one you craved. You were
given the gift of mercy.
—Perhaps it was harsh—
—Perhaps it was severe—
But mercy nonetheless."

Mercy? How could you call that mercy? Something so brutally painful!

"Of course it hurt.
It will continue to hurt for
some time still, but you
have the chance to do better.
How much more severe
would it be to allow you to go
on clinging to that poor wild
baby, making it your creature
when it should be free—when you
should be free from a need
that is slowly killing you?"

I'm a mother. How can I be free of the need to nurture? It's who I am, and what could be more honorable and appropriate?

"I see what you're doing.
You know you weren't
really nurturing him.
Otherwise, it wouldn't
hurt so much to think
about him."

But what is the point? Why him? Why now?

"Blaise, of course."

My real baby. I should have been mothering him right now . . . I should've been allowed . . .

"You think you can say
what *should* have been?
Let them go. That's the
lesson—let them go.
You hold so tightly
to things that can only
hold you back. You
have to struggle on."

I don't want to struggle! I want to be with them! I want to love them!

"If you love them,
you'll keep struggling.
You'll let them go."
The soft voice was pleasant
and really seemed to know.

"Well, that was a load
of jackrabbit turds.
You know that you should
be with them. Why should
you have to be without
them, or they without you?
It's unnatural and cruel!
They need you. You're
the Mother, after all!
It wasn't fair or just!"
The first voice had returned,
and it really seemed to know . . .

Yes . . . that's true . . . I am the Mother.

"If you'd been allowed

to keep them, you wouldn't
have made the same mistake
as you did with Baby.
You wouldn't have smothered
Blaise . . . or the other one if
it had lived."

She—if she had lived. And no, I wouldn't have! I was a good mother! I
deserved to keep them!

"Then again . . . you *are* the Mother
of Wild Beasts. It's who you are,
remember? You'd have made him
tasty desert cakes out of the foods
you neglected to teach him how to
forage for himself. Then one day,
you wouldn't be there for him.
He'd die like Baby, and it would be all
your fault. So sad . . . so sad . . ."

What? No!

"Don't listen to that rubbish,"
the softer voice said. "What might
have been has no more reality
than a mirage in the distance.
It doesn't do to dwell on what
might have been. And anyway,
you *can* change! You can be
transfigured and healed and whole!
It's why you're here!

"You can't change, and what's more
you don't have to. You are what you
are—and so what if you were to smother
your own child the way you smothered
that stolen kitten? Think how it made
you feel to care for him! To *kill* for him!

I won't do that again! Never! And I wouldn't have done that with Blaise!

"You are what you are. Isn't that what
you've always said? That you love
your child *fiercely*? You can do no
different. It's your destiny and your
identity. She would have you neglect
your own children and your own identity!
What else do you have in this world?
What about *your* needs?
You need to be needed, and there's
nothing wrong with that! Nothing
wrong with you! It was all just
completely unjust and undeserved!"

"Letting go in due season is not neglect.
The true test of motherlove
is to let them go when the time
is right. It's not for you to decide
what season is right for them
to go—what age, or how or where.
He is gone for now, and you must
let him go and carry on."

Oh, stop it! Both of you! Stop, stop, stop, and just . . . just stop talking! I need quiet! I need to think! Just . . . stop it! I really couldn't afford to lose so much moisture, but the tears wouldn't stop. They were as relentless as the voices that tormented me.

"Magda . . .you're so tired.
You've been through more
than is fair or just. It's time
to say goodbye to this painful
life. Nothing good can come
of it. You have lost everything
of value and comfort to you.
It's time—here—under the Ironwood
tree— it's time to kill yourself"
the first voice said very kindly . . .
very gently . . . and it really
 did seem to know . . .

5

Visitation

"Why are you crying?" I heard the voice—the softer second voice—trying to break into the conversation again.

"Why are you crying?" I heard it say again. As if it didn't know! The voices arguing inside my head all heard each other. I ignored its stupid question.

"Why are you crying?" Why was it pretending to be so obtuse?

"Why are you crying?" Why would it not give up and leave me alone?

"Why are you crying?" The voice was so persistent, the thought finally dawned on me, slowly: might this voice be *outside*? Might it actually have stepped beyond the thronging forum that my mind had become? I painfully drew my aching eyelids up, barely high enough to check. I saw against the blinding glare of the sun, a woman's form in silhouette.

"Who are you?" I whispered.

"Why are you crying?" the stranger asked again. She wouldn't give up that one question.

"The voices," I responded weakly.

"What do they tell you to do?" My eyes welled up again with more of those precious tears that mustn't be wasted.

"One of them told me to make it end—my life—to kill myself."

"You're nearly dead already, I'm afraid," the stranger said. "I told you you need to find a well."

"That was you?" I asked, opening my half-shut eyes a fraction wider, trying to see the stranger more clearly. What I saw was a wild woman, gaunt and bony and brown. She was nearly naked, and by her side, docile as a kitten, sat a massive mountain lion. "Who are you?"

"I don't matter. I'm just a handmaiden. What does matter is that you will die very shortly. You're dying now, my dear, and it's closer than you think."

"I know I am . . . I feel that it's close. But what can be done? Maybe to die is better anyway . . ."

"Certainly, one's death is precious, to be guarded and kept for its proper time. But the proper time isn't for you to simply choose as you wish."

"It's too late . . . isn't it," I whispered.

"It's not," the stranger insisted. "Get up. Walk due East from this point until you reach a low wall with a little gate. Pull the bell and wait. But you have to go now. Go!"

"But how long . . ." I had only turned my head to look to the East, but when I turned again to the strange woman, she was gone without a trace. Only the tracks of an enormous cat remained in the sand. I drew a painful breath that burned my nostrils and ached in my throat and chest. I rose and started walking slowly East.

How I made it was a mystery. How I kept walking when my body was shutting down from dehydration and hunger, I will never know. I wasn't sure if I was dead, dreaming, or really arriving at the little low wall with its blue gate and its bell-pull swaying in the breeze. With the last of my strength, I grabbed the rope, trusting it to be real and not just a mirage. I grabbed the rope, and the last thing I heard was the clear, deep-throated voice of the clanging bell.

I don't remember how I got from that moment at the gate to the moment when I woke up indoors, in a bed, with a cool cup of water next to me. What was this place? I didn't seem to be dead. I seemed to be better! I sat up and looked out the little window. There was a garden in view and a few darkly clad female figures tending it. And then a knock on the door.

"You're awake!" A round, gentle-looking female face peered in at me.

"Am I? I'm not so sure," I said. "Where am I?"

"You're in our garden."

"Strange place for a garden."

"Not really. In fact, we think there's no better place."

"How did you get here?" I asked.

"We came. All from different places."

"On purpose?" I asked incredulously.

"For whatever reason, we all decided it was where we needed to be. How did you get here?" she asked kindly.

"I don't know. I just woke up here. It wasn't on purpose, and I'd leave right now if I could."

"Why?"

"Well . . . because it's terrible."

"Why?"

"It's lonely—it's dry—it's just empty, you know?"

"No, I don't understand."

"Well, obviously, since you're here with other people . . . how did you manage that?"

"We're a desert community. We do have each other, and yet we don't. We belong to each other, and yet we don't. It's a little hard to describe. There are seasons when we go out of the garden and into the badlands alone. But we always come back at the appointed time. Where are you from? You say you woke up here?"

"I was exiled. My family was taken from me."

"I see. And now you find yourself wandering here—looking for something?"

"Yes."

"Do you know what it is?"

"I have an inkling."

"Describe it to me."

"Well, in the deep desert, there is very little water. I've gotten it only occasionally and at great effort when I'm nearly convinced I'm dying. I'm looking for a constant source—a well."

"Excellent."

"You know of one?"

"Yes, of course."

"Well, where is it?"

"It's here."

"Here?" I sat up with excitement.

Yes, that's why we built our garden here."

"Well, that's good news! Can I see it?"

"I don't know."

"What do you mean?"

"Well, it's hard to see unless you have eyes to see it."

"I have eyes."

"Yes, to be sure, but there's a lot of sand in them, after all."

"No, there isn't. I can see just fine," I argued.

"My dear girl . . ." the woman said with concern. "My dear, dear girl . . ."

"No, really—I can see the spider up in the corner—that little crack in the plaster . . ." The woman just chuckled. "Why are you laughing?"

"Just stay here a while, if you can bear to. You may yet catch sight of that well you're looking for."

"May I?"

"You may, but understand that there is no Utopia out here awaiting your discovery. This is the desert. We're here for one purpose and one purpose only."

"What is that?"

"To mourn, to heal, and to become human, of course."

"I'm human already. I just want to leave here—to be in a place where it's easier to live more comfortably. I want to be with my family. Anything is better than where I've been," I said.

"Don't be so sure."

"Well, isn't there anything else out there?"

"There's just the desert. More and more dry sand without end—and mirages."

"I'm here permanently?"

"Well, nothing under the power of Time is really permanent, is it?" She wasn't as simple as she seemed.

"But life is so hard in the desert . . ." I mused, half to myself.

"If it was easy, it would be empty."

"To me it *is* empty. Empty and inhospitable."

"The desert is beautiful. Like the little prince told the stranded pilot—'what makes the desert beautiful is that somewhere it hides a well.' Just be still a while. Don't settle for the shallow wells you dig yourself. They can't last. You'll reach the bottom before you've had your fill. You must become an archeologist and uncover wells much older than you or me."

"I really don't know what you mean." I did, but I didn't want to admit it.

"Just be still. Wait. Be watchful, and just wait."

"I don't know what I'm watching for." At least that was true.

"You'll know it when you see it."

"What do I do until then?"

"Do?"

"Well, I have to do something, don't I?"

"Just be silent. Work in the garden. Listen. Watch. Wait."

"And did you stay?" Summer asked.

"Hm? Oh yes. Yes, I stayed. I worked and listened and learned a great deal . . . then I left. I've often wished I hadn't, but it's so very hard to detach from some things . . . so very hard. And there has always been this one thing, you know? This one thing I just can't shake—can't give up."

"And what's that?" Magda just smiled, and Summer blushed, realizing how personal her question must have been. "Well, I don't see why you should have to detach from everything. What's wrong with attachment if the object itself is good? Why should you approach all the good in this life with indifference? How does that help anything?"

"Detachment and indifference are different."

"I don't think so. I think the one leads to the other. Detachment leads to indifference and indifference to detachment."

"Not necessarily. You can love something without being attached to it. Care deeply for it without having to possess it. I can look at a flower, appreciate it, even give it a drink of water, yet resist the urge to pick it and make it mine. If I'm detached, it doesn't mean I don't care. It means I'm free from need and love the other enough to leave it free as well."

"But what's so wrong with need? Babies attach to their mothers because they need them, after all."

"For a time, yes—for a season. It's an attachment that changes, loosens as the child grows. It is not out of indifference that the mother bird pushes its chick from the nest. It's to show the fledgling how strong her own wings have become. An oppressive need to nurture can lead nowhere good. Think of Baby—think of Cat, Summer." Summer's ears turned pink.

"You think I'm oppressive? We need each other. I was lonely, she needed a home . . . our needs aligned. We're good for each other—you've said so yourself."

"It's good for you to have someone, it's true. But beware of anything that brings you more worry than peace."

"Everyone worries over the things they love most."

"No, Summer. People like you and me do that because we've lost so much. We've loved too hard, hoped too hard, and we've taken the wrong lesson from our loss."

"What lesson can there be in loss like ours? It's senseless!"

"The same lesson we will continue to have thrust upon us until we learn it: that the way forward is the way of dispossession—relinquishing our need to possess another soul to obsess over and fuss over while ignoring our own disease: our need to need and be needed."

"I don't need that. I just need to be with you in your garden."

"You need *me*?"

"To be with you in your garden. You're teaching me things I can't understand, but I need to know them, I feel . . . I know that they're true."

"I'm not sure you should be alone . . . but I'm not sure you should be with me either. You need to be where I was, but maybe do what I couldn't and stay. I'm no elder, Summer. No sage counselor. I'm just a wanderer like you. I've only wandered longer."

6

The House

Magda was good at speaking in enigmas. What did it all mean? What was it all for in the end? These mysterious monologues—ramblings that said nothing and everything. Summer had been sure only a few weeks ago that Magda was a tragic genius telling her life in poetry, but these voices! Summer didn't like them. They worried her beyond anything else that was causing her anxiety that fall, or even that year! She was still convinced that Magda was some sort of brilliant philosopher, poet, and sage whose wisdom she wanted to absorb, but those voices—voices, unanswered questions, and omitted details. Perhaps it wasn't a question of Magda being mad or sane, healthy or unhealthy. Perhaps she was somehow both at once—but which parts were which?

Summer sat in her accustomed spot, tucked into the shoulder of her red sofa, enjoying the first real fire of the fall season. It wasn't really cold enough for a fire yet, but with the maple trees starting to tinge at the edges and a light misty rain falling that evening, she couldn't resist. How it filled the room! It was like a living, breathing being that changed color with every heaving breath. An empty house was the hardest thing about living on her own. Cat had helped alleviate her loneliness, and the fire, once really lit and not just in the form of sad little pine-scented candles, lent the room a peculiar fullness. Summer took comfort from its undulating orange embers and wondered. How had Magda lived all these years by herself, alone in that house without even a pet for company? Unless one counted a metaphorical bobcat kitten that seemed to represent . . .well, she still wasn't absolutely sure what it represented. Had other neighbors sat with her under the apple tree and heard her strange stories? Or had everyone else avoided Crazy Magda and left her to her own mysterious devices?

All alone in that house . . . Summer had never been inside, but she had imagined what it must be like. A fire in the hearth makes curious thoughts all the more vivid, and by that first fire of autumn, Summer imagined Magda's house. How cozy she must have made it to live there so contentedly by herself.

Summer had never really known her grandparents. They had all died within a few years of each other when she was very young, but she did have a hazy memory of visiting her father's mother when she must have been no older than five. She remembered patterned afghans and doilies, ceramic figurines, the smell of coffee and cigarettes mingling with the scent of potpourri, spaghetti sauce, and garlic bread. There was a black long-haired cat that wouldn't let her pet it. It hissed at her from under a rose-colored velvet chair with feet like a lion. The old mantle clock ticked out of sync with the cuckoo clock on the wall. She remembered rushing over to watch the cuckoo come out of hiding when the hour struck.

Summer decided that Magda's house must be something like that, but better. She was certain Magda didn't smoke, so, minus the cigarette smell, she pictured her home as being at least similar to her memories of her grandmother's house. Old things—the quirky little artifacts one keeps not because they are valuable but because they remind you of someone you once loved. Knick-knacks that hold a hundred stories and memories— the smell of something cooking—black and white pictures of weddings, christenings, bearded patriarchs, and grim-faced matriarchs. What stories would Magda tell inside her house? Maybe she would tell them straight, instead of making metaphors and poetry to tell things that never quite added up. Summer wanted to see it. She wanted to see inside the house.

. . . why had Magda never invited her in?

Summer knit her brow and rose from her cozy spot by the fire. Yes— why had Magda never invited her inside her house? Why, even in the winter, had they only ever met in the garden? Was she hiding something? Did she not trust Summer? Maybe she was a hoarder! Maybe she had a hundred cats! Perhaps she had her dead husband taxidermied and propped up in his favorite chair with a 45-year-old newspaper placed in a shiny lacquered hand . . . okay, now that was just crazy! But maybe she never cleaned . . . though her garden was so neat and tidy, Summer could hardly imagine that her home would be any less meticulously cared for.

Why would she not invite her in? Was it something about Summer? Was she not as close of a friend as she thought? She considered the old woman to be family—her closest friend. Maybe Magda didn't feel the same. If she did, surely she would have invited her into her home by now.

The mystery of Magda's home grew to epic proportions in Summer's imagination as she paced the fire-lit, flickering, breathing, living room—as though she were pacing the convolutions of her own brain, each spark from the fire representing a firing synapse. She was exploring the maze of her own thoughts, trying different scenarios against what she knew about Magda and her past, feeling that just around some mental bend, the obvious answer was waiting.

Perhaps Magda was just incredibly private and didn't want to share her space with anyone. But even that didn't make sense. She shared everything. She shared every kind of produce from her garden with Summer, with the neighbors, even with the mail carrier. What could possibly be in that house that she wouldn't want anyone else to see? The only obvious answer Summer discovered that evening, lurking around a corner in her mind, was the existence of something she wanted most in all the world yet hadn't realized until that very moment: to go inside Magda's house and snoop.

How could she manage such an infiltration . . . and was it right? She loved Magda and wanted to respect her privacy, but she also wanted to see inside her house. It wasn't idle curiosity, after all. It was surely just healthy, friendly, totally justified interest. She could just ask. Yes, maybe she should just ask Magda to show her the inside of the house. She could be interested in seeing the house that Maxim built. That would be upfront and direct, and honest. Surely, Magda wouldn't deny her. But every time Summer tried to think up the right, naturally phrased request, it sounded creepy and invasive. What was wrong with her! Surely anyone else could ask to see her house without sounding like a stalker!

Maybe she could just go in one day—looking for something. Yes, looking for something that would be totally normal. A tissue or a glass of water. Yes, a glass of water would be perfect! She would bake something to take with her. Something that made one thirsty. Scones! While Magda was busy in the garden. She could just say—not ask—just say, "I'm going to get a drink of water" and just go in. That way, she could see what Magda would do. Would she try to prevent her? Say something like, "oh no . . . I'll get you one—you wait out here" or some other excuse? That would be a valuable experiment. She would try it. She would try it tomorrow!

7

The Desert Cave

Summer awoke that morning with an unsettled stomach—the kind she would get before exams, presentations, or answering the phone. She was nervous but determined. Today she would see the inside of Magda's house! Maybe—unless Magda had something to hide, in which case she would find that out instead, which was also valuable. She got through her day in distracted indifference, reading over case studies, discussing them with only shallow observations to share, then she rushed home to put her plan into action.

Summer went straight to her kitchen and baked scones—plain ones—no fruit or anything to give them extra moisture, and she certainly wouldn't take butter or jam! They had to make them both awfully thirsty. She took the scones out of the oven and put them on a plate, still piping hot. Everything was set. She stepped out the door and crossed over into Magda's front yard. Everything was just as Summer had imagined it in her mind. Magda was there, in her garden as usual. Summer poked her head over the gate and greeted her. Magda, as usual, motioned her in, pointing her to the bench under the apple tree.

"It's such a beautiful day!" Summer said. "Fall is here! I can feel it!"

"Oh yes, it's certainly coming. I could smell it last night—did you have a fire?"

"I did! It was absolutely wonderful!"

"I also heard your air conditioner running."

"Well . . . yeah, I know it's not really fire weather yet. I just couldn't wait! And look! I've made scones! They're hot from the oven!"

"Lovely! You go ahead and have one. I'm not quite finished in my pumpkin patch, but I'll be over to join you in a few minutes."

This was better than Summer could have hoped for. The pumpkin patch was on the other side of the house. She could just go into the house through the screen porch, and Magda wouldn't even see her! If she did, the glass of water was still a valid excuse. Summer waited, nibbling nervously at one of the dry, crumbly scones until Magda's silver braids and green beanie disappeared around the side of the house, then she rose from the bench. Her legs felt heavy and stiff like they felt when getting up to give presentations in school. She took a deep breath, walked up to the back door, and turned the knob.

***

Summer blamed herself, of course, for not having been more curious about Magda's living arrangements sooner. She had only assumed that the wholesome, meticulously cared for garden with its bounty and beauty must be simply an extension of a tastefully furnished, homey living space, full of warmth and comfort. She had pictured country-style handmade quilts, indoor plants as lovingly doted upon as the ones out in the garden. She had imagined antique feather beds on frames perhaps made by Magda's late husband, china cabinets filled with ceramic bird sculptures, fancy teacups, and other family heirlooms that Magda had cherished all her long life—each with its own story over which she might linger in the telling on a wet evening with a cup of tea. She had expected old family pictures on the walls—pictures of Maxim and Blaise—still life paintings of flowers and fruit, framed cross-stitch quotations about the joys of family life, maybe a record player to fill her nights with nostalgic music, and a cozy old-fashioned chair like the one her grandmother had might sit by the window, overlooking her beloved garden.

How she had let herself imagine that space, down to the long, polished dining table with a bowl of roses or lilacs or whatever was blooming. How she had convinced herself that it would smell like baking bread, stewing fruit, and cinnamon. Summer had so easily invented this magical, grandmotherly space for Magda because Magda seemed to be so magical and grandmotherly herself—kind of like the grandmother Summer remembered meeting, but much, much better and without a mean cat waiting to hiss and swipe at her. Yet why had it taken her so long to wonder why they always sat in the garden when she visited—why they always chatted outside, or in her own living room but never inside Magda's home. Now Summer stood on the threshold, surveying the reality of Magda's life, feeling her chest begin to constrict and reaching with a practiced gesture for her vial of lavender oil.

It's not that it was dirty or even disorderly. There weren't hordes of cats or stacks of mail or decades' worth of old newspapers piled up along the walls and stacked up on moldering furniture. There was no taxidermized husband or even a favorite chair for him to sit upon with his yellowed paper. There was nothing—absolutely nothing. The house was empty.

Summer tried the light switch. The house had no power. It didn't make sense—how was it that light glowed from the windows all night? Did she have candles? A flashlight or a lantern? Summer rushed into the kitchen and flung open the cabinets. Nothing! Nothing but a few empty canning jars. What was keeping this woman alive? The bedrooms were likewise bare. Not only were there no charming handmade quilts on antique feather beds, but there were no beds at all. No blankets. No pillows. No evidence that anyone ever entered that house, except for the absence of dust and spider webs. It was at least immaculately clean.

By now, Summer was beyond panicking and actually starting to be angry. Angry at the old woman for letting her eat her pecans and pickles, and peaches and other garden produce when it was obviously all she lived on. Angry at herself for not being nosier and making sure she had what she needed—that she had power to heat and cool her home and a bed to sleep in. This was not acceptable!

What could she do? What *should* she do? Summer's first instinct was to take Magda home with her then and there. Have her sleep in her own bed while Summer slept on the sofa. In her heart, she knew Magda would never allow it. She would never take more of anything, never take comfort at the expense of someone else. Still, maybe she would sleep on the sofa. Even that would be better than sleeping on the floor in a cold empty house. Summer couldn't be sure, but she had to assume that was how Magda had been sleeping, for who knew how long.

There still remained the problem of that house. *The* house. The house that Maxim built. The house she had lived in with her little boy and her husband. The one with the garden and the little cairn of stones in the corner. The only link she still had to them—to her lost loves. Summer knew she would never leave it, even to sleep next door. And anyway, Summer was young—just starting out in life—was it fair that she be saddled with such a responsibility when she really ought to be free? Free to learn and explore and become? Free from worry for someone who wasn't even hers by blood to worry about? Surely . . .

Summer kept mulling these questions and options over in her mind as she surveyed the lonely dark cave that she had never known Magda's home to be. She was old. She was odd. She grew more and more strange with the passage of time, and the neighbors had already complained. She'd already been taken away once. Something had to be done—for her own health—for her own safety. This odd little life she'd been secretly leading couldn't be allowed to continue this way. It just wasn't right—it just wasn't healthy. Summer felt it would come down to her, the one who knew this woman best—the one who knew she was harmless and good—the one who was already trusted and held power of attorney and official guardianship. She would have to be the one to make the hard decision on Magda's behalf. Summer's heartbeat quickened, and the walls felt as though they were closing in on her as she felt the weight of Magda's future in her hands.

"Are you looking for something?" Summer turned and saw Magda standing behind her. The old woman wasn't angry—she didn't even seem embarrassed by her home—she just looked at Summer with her usual sparse smile. Summer was so upset that she forgot her lie about getting water.

"Magda . . . I'm sorry. I was curious."

"It's all right. You've never been inside my house before. Did you find what you were looking for?"

"Well, not really."

"Come in. Come and sit."

"Sit? Where?"

"Oh anywhere. Anywhere is fine. I like the spot by the window." She pointed to the back window facing the garden. Summer wanted to yell. She wanted to scold the old woman for living such a secretly austere life. She got hold of herself and searched her repertoire of rhetorical strategies for extracting information without apparent judgment and without asking for it directly.

"Tell me about your home, Magda."

"Well, you can see for yourself now."

"I'd still like to hear about it from you."

"Well, it's lovely, isn't it? Maxim made it for us. He made it with his own hands. We filled it with love . . . so very much love, and music, and laughter, and dancing! My little Blaise was born in this house."

"Not in the hospital?"

"Oh no. Blaise was born at home, away from all the sick people. Maxim and I delivered him together, and he was such a healthy, beautiful boy! I used to rock him in the evenings while the mockingbird still sang its song at the top of the tree by his window . . . the old pecan tree. It was smaller then."

"What happened to all of your things?"

"I didn't need them."

"What do you mean you didn't need them? You didn't need a place to sit? A place to sleep?"

"You'd be surprised how little you really need. I renounced it. I let it all go. All but this house . . ." She looked down at the floor with a strange expression. Was it shame? "I've held on to it. It's so hard to . . ."

"What?"

"Well, I've tried to detach myself from it. I spend less and less time in it. I sleep in the garden now except in wet weather."

"You *what*?" Summer couldn't hide her shock, try as she might to seem calm and unfazed. It would have been easier to pretend if she didn't care so much—love so much. Magda saw her uneasiness and paused, sensing perhaps that she had said too much.

"I'm happy now, you know? I was so low for so long . . . my exile was painful—very painful—but it got better. I was fed. I was watered. I was transported. I was planted in this garden, and I've grown a bit. It has grown me, and I know I haven't grown any fruits yet, but I hope to soon."

Summer didn't reply. In her mind and heart, she had made certain discoveries . . . had certain realizations. It gave her pain, but she knew it had to be. If she didn't make the decision, then someone who cared for Magda less would make it for her, and with less consideration. Summer was convinced now that Magda's dementia—yes, she believed now that she could call it dementia—was more advanced than she had ever guessed and that she was a danger to herself. The time had come for her to be cared for by professionals—people who could give her the safe environment she needed—the nourishment, comfort, and care to which her age and situation had entitled her. It was time. It was well and truly time.

8

The Decision

It wasn't difficult to arrange Magda's new situation at the nursing home. Summer already had guardianship over her, and within a few days, she had found a place that seemed decent enough and was ready to take her immediately. The problem that ate at her insides and robbed her of sleep at night was how she would actually break it to Magda and how she would get her there. Would she come willingly? Would there be an ugly scene? Would she resist?

Maybe Summer could offer to take Magda on a drive somewhere. It would have to be somewhere very tempting considering that Magda hadn't voluntarily ridden in a car since that fateful accident that took her husband and son away from her. Since then, she had seemingly only ridden in police cars. What might be compelling enough to tempt her into the car willingly?

"Magda," Summer asked her that Saturday morning from over the top of the fence, "would you like to come on a walk through the preserve today? It's safe to take walks, and we can bring masks with us just in case we pass someone on a narrower trail. It's nice and cool now, and the trees are starting to turn. The last time I went, I saw a great blue heron, and it was hunting for little fish in the pond."

"Drive to the preserve with you in your car?"

"Yes, you can see where I like to take Cat walking. I don't think I'll take her this time. She tends to scare the birds and bark at the squirrels. It might be nice to have a walk there, just the two of us. There's an incredible climbing tree there. A massive old magnolia! I haven't been up it myself, but I've seen some kids climbing it. Really a very impressive tree. You should see it."

"I haven't been there since . . . I used to take Blaise there. I believe we even climbed that tree of yours, though it's probably much bigger now."

"Oh . . . I didn't know. Never mind. Forget I asked. Of course, you don't want to go there again. I'm sorry."

"No . . ." Magda paused, looking at Summer with growing determination in her eyes. "No, I want to go with you. I want to go in your car—go see that place again—see the tree and the heron. Take me with you whenever it's convenient for you. I'll put my work aside when you're ready." Summer hadn't dared hope for such a response.

"This afternoon? After lunch?" she asked.

"Yes. Yes, I'll come with you. Come for me whenever you're ready."

At least that part had proved easier than expected. Summer felt a sickening mixture of satisfaction and guilt rising up in her stomach like bile. She ran to the house and drank down a glass of water. She lay on the sofa for a moment, trying to determine what words she could possibly say to Magda when she didn't take her back home after their walk—when they arrived at the nursing home—when she left her there committed to the care of strangers without any warning or preparation. Maybe she should have talked with her first—given her some warning. Maybe that would have been fair, but something in her prevented that discussion. She couldn't seem to produce the words, and the time was never right.

She had spent sleepless nights leading up to this day, deliberating over the decision and trying to imagine a scenario where she had the courage to tell Magda what she'd decided for her. She had begun clenching her teeth and having neck spasms from the anxiety of her responsibility for Magda's future. Still, she was convinced that Magda needed looking after by people who knew what they were doing and did it professionally. Magda wasn't thinking clearly enough to make that decision for herself, and it was Summer's responsibility to do the thinking for her this time and get her the care she needed.

Summer sat that morning, all tension and nerves, almost wishing it was she—she who would go and be cared for and have good decisions made on her behalf. How pleasant it must be to be looked after—to let someone else do her thinking for her, at least for a little while, until she felt better. She was so exhausted, worn weary through anxiety over things beyond her control—the ever-present threat of the virus, her classes, her future, the future of the nation gearing up for elections, and of course now Magda—Magda's future.

Yes, if only someone else could think for her, just for a day—maybe two—a short vacation from the constant ruckus of her thoughts and worries. But that would be impossible. Not that there was any shortage of people out there who were more than willing to take charge of her thoughts, but she knew that she would return only to find that she'd joined a cult or bought expensive life-insurance or become embroiled in some sort of pyramid scheme involving weight loss drinks. No, the closest she could get to a break from her own clamoring thoughts was that little orange bottle in her medicine cabinet. She'd opened it only twice before—right after her time in the emergency room.

It frightened her. That's why she was so reluctant to open it again—swallow its contents and accept the temporary relief it offered. It frightened her how much she enjoyed the break from her thoughts, and she feared that she might get used it—prefer it even—that quiet, muffled state, as though her mind were wrapped up in a warm, wool blanket and that nothing unpleasant could penetrate it, at least for a few hours. No, that pill was only to take away her worst anxiety—the kind that escalated into panic.

But that pill did more than stop the approaching freight train of panic. It gave Summer a break from herself—her own incessant voice blathering away in her head about everything and nothing—reminding her of stupid things she'd said in high school. Most of the time, it felt as though she was living in a documentary, where she was simultaneously the rare bird under observation and the naturalist narrating its behaviors, its eating habits, and its plumage. How miserable to live in a constant state of self-consciousness—self-analysis—self-diagnosis. But how much worse to need a pill just to escape one's own internal monologue. How sad. Too sad. Too sad to be indulged.

No, she would breathe deep her lavender oil, soak in her bath salts, light her comforting fireplace candles, hug her dog, and continue to do her own thinking. She must. And now she must think for Magda too. It was best this way—no deliberation or discussion. No argument. It was done. Still, it did seem as if some explanation was merited—why so suddenly Magda was being uprooted. A letter—that was it.

Summer would write it all down in a letter so that there would be no chance of her forgetting to say all the things she meant to promise Magda—about the frequency with which she would come and visit her—about how she would care for her garden and bring her things from it—about how she would arrange to bring Cat to see her and bring her homemade baked goods every weekend. She would write about how Magda wouldn't have to sleep on the ground or go days without speaking to other people—and there would be people there—people who could help her if she needed anything. If she was ever hungry, cold, afraid—there would always be help. Yes, that was it. She must write Magda a letter that contained all that she was feeling—all the ways she was prepared to make it up to her.

Summer pulled herself together and made a trip to the store to buy a few essential items for Magda, knowing now how little she had to bring with her. She purchased her an overnight bag, a soft nightgown with flowers on it, some slippers, a comfortable new outfit, socks, underwear, and toiletries. That would be enough for now. She could always get more things later as needs arose. She paused in the toy department. Her eyes were drawn to the stuffed animals. She thought she might send a teddy bear with her, but none of them were smiling for some odd reason, so she didn't end up buying one. Magda wouldn't want a stuffed bear anyway, let alone a frowning one. What was she thinking?

When Summer returned home, she carefully clipped all the price tags from the new items and folded them neatly, packing them inside the overnight bag. Then she sat down at her desk with a sheet of paper and a pen.

> Dear Magda,
> I know what you must be thinking right now, and I'm so very sorry I've had to do this . . .

No, that wasn't right.

> My Dearest Friend,
> A time comes in every person's life when we must accept the coming of age with grace and dignity . . .

That was wrong, too—even worse than the first.

> My Dearest Magda,
> I will miss talking with you in the garden every day, seeing your face over the fence. I will miss having you close, but I will visit you as much as I can. A few times a week, at least. I will take care of your garden and pick things to bring you when they are ripe. I will bring Cat with me to see you, too, if they will let me. I brought you here because I—

Summer paused, mulling over the words she was about to write. They were true. She knew they were, but they had only come to her in that moment, and their force surprised her.

I brought you here because I love you. I cannot bear to think of you sleeping in your garden, not having a warm, safe bed, a place to sit, or attention from people who know how and what kind of care you might need. Please don't be angry with your girl. This decision has been hard, and I simply see no other way. I promise with all my heart that it is for the best. I will be back to visit soon.
Love,
Your Girl Summer

Summer folded the letter carefully, creasing the edges sharp with her fingernail, and placed it atop the new floral nightgown in the new overnight bag. She paused, looking at it a moment before finally drawing a deep breath and zipping the bag shut.

9

The Old Magnolia

They strolled together arm in arm, through the meadow, past the creek, under the arching foliage. Magda stopped every few seconds to examine an insect, a mushroom, a moss, a fringe of lichen, a fallen leaf tinged with orange. She saw everything before Summer did, despite Summer's younger, sharper eyes—despite her heightened powers of observation, so carefully cultivated. She saw the great blue heron, still as a statue, waiting to spear a fish—heard every bird's song and knew its name without having to see it.

Summer wasn't really there. She nodded to Magda's comments about the delicate pattern of the dead cicada's wing, like fracture glass. She looked into the hunting heron's keen eye but didn't really see or appreciate it. She stood and seemed to observe the swallows swooping over the pond, feasting on a cloud of tiny insects, but all she saw was the picture in her mind—a picture of herself trying to explain to Magda why she wasn't taking her back home. The kingfisher laughed, but all she heard were the words of her letter, the words of their parting—her reassurances and excuses.

They crossed the suspension bridge over the creek. Summer's thoughts were likewise suspended, stretched between past and future. Only Magda seemed to be fully and joyfully present. How long must it have been since Magda had been anywhere but her own neighborhood? Her childlike joy only made Summer feel worse about what she was going to do after their walk. They reached the tree—the one Blaise used to climb—the old magnolia with low slung arms outstretched in friendly invitation. Magda ran her hand over its bark slowly, tenderly.

"I don't usually meet anyone more ancient than me anymore, old friend. Look how you've grown! You were just beginning to be a fine climbing tree the last time I saw you but look at you now! You're magnificent! You must be nearing the end, like me." Summer was standing at the edge of the pond, looking out at the water, barely listening to Magda's reminiscences. All she heard was the mental cacophony of optional explanations for why she was committing Magda to the care of others—staged conversations and possible responses.

"I don't have a boy to climb you anymore—that's why I haven't been back to visit before now. I mostly spend my time throwing rocks at demons and trying to help this poor girl whose mind is injured by anger and grief. Don't worry, she's not listening. She usually isn't. She's in the past, holding her lost sister . . . or in the future, being important and saving the day. She's very young. I've been trying to help her. What she needs is a big, old tree like you to show her how to be still and acquire peace! I'm not a tree. I can't teach her much. I just tell her stories. I thought a paradox might wake her up, but she places everything real and vital about my stories in a tidy little compartment for things she calls myths and folklore and metaphors and delusions.

"She thinks she wants to learn how to be in the desert full-time, like the cactus wren or the mourning dove, but I think she really just doesn't like people very much. People scare her. She thinks they judge her. She thinks they're all better, smarter, richer, more educated, more attractive . . . maybe she wants to help people because she wants to feel superior to them for once . . . you know, I think I might just climb you, for old time's sake . . ." Magda began to carefully make her way up the tree, while Summer stared unseeing at the turtles in the pond.

"That's better. I can see everything more clearly from up here. You've filled out quite nicely, haven't you! I remember your limbs used to bend a little when I climbed you, but now you're solid as a rock! Barely a tremble! I've gotten more solid as well. I was bent—nearly snapped in two when I lost them. I was thinner then—more brittle and porous. Things seeped in so easily. Worry. Anger. The voices . . . It's not that they've gone away, you know, I just know what to do about them now. Where to go for help. I've been cared for very gently through all of this. The voices still come, but His is louder."

"Magda! You shouldn't be up there! You could fall!" Summer, having turned and noticed Magda yards above her head in the dark, shiny foliage of the old magnolia, raced up the tree after her.

"You see what I mean? She's coming to my rescue!"

"You should care for yourself better! What if you fell?"

"I've fallen countless times, Summer. I would do what I always do: get up and try again."

"You could break a bone so easily! You shouldn't be climbing trees at your age."

"I should be climbing more and higher, but I've grown tired. Maybe I've gone as far as I can go, but I know others who have gone much farther."

"It's not safe up here."

"It's not safe down there."

"It's time to go."

"Is that really for you to say?"

"I'm the one with the car. Now come down out of the tree, very carefully. Watch where I step and follow me down."

"No, you follow me up."

"Don't be stubborn, Magda. It's high time you acted your age."

"Listen to her! She's grown so much older than you or me, poor thing! I could just weep!"

"I'm serious, Magda. We're leaving now."

Summer and Magda climbed down from the old magnolia tree, and Summer breathed a deep sigh of relief that Magda was still in one piece and not scratched or bruised, potentially exposing her to awkward questions when she delivered Magda to the nursing home. This only confirmed to Summer's mind that she was right in getting her friend professional care. Magda was becoming a danger to herself, and Summer wouldn't always be there to help her. They walked back to the car, Magda prattling on about something or other, and Summer scowling deeply, hearing nothing, still trying to decide on the right words to leave Magda at their parting. They climbed into the car, and Summer drove Magda to her new home.

10

The First Visit

Magda hadn't said a word. She hadn't seemed surprised or even apprehensive. She watched Summer patiently as she recited her rehearsed explanation and then watched her leave. Summer felt foolish for having expected a scene. Whatever befell her, Magda never seemed to get angry but shook her green beanie and silver braids with that jack-o-lantern grin of hers and simply carried on.

Still, Summer feared that first visit to the nursing home. She feared Magda's anger might have been slow to come but grew after Summer had left her there and as the realization of her new situation dawned. Summer feared that this decision, made on her behalf without consultation or warning, would mean the end of their friendship as it had been. More than anything, she feared losing Magda, who had become to her something unexpected: a window and a mirror—her crazy stories, her endless babbling song, her garden—had all become a means by which Summer finally began to see herself and catch a glimpse of what she could be. She had come to need the old woman's stories and friendship, where she had always thought it was Crazy Magda who needed her. It was with a trembling hand and pounding heart that she turned the knob and opened the door to Magda's room.

The first sight to meet Summer was the soft floral nightgown she'd packed for Magda and a pair of shuffling slippered feet. The face, however, gave Summer an unexpected shock. It was pale and drawn, creased with age and pain, and it frowned at her with deep distrust. It wasn't Magda at all. Someone else, some stranger, was in Magda's clothes . . . in Magda's room.

"Oh! Hello there . . ." Summer said gently.

"You get out of here! Out! You're not welcome here!" the woman yelled, clutching at the back of a chair to steady herself.

"My name is Summer. I'm looking for Magda."

"I know who you are! I know what you're here for! I said get out! I have a gun!" Summer ducked out of the room and walked briskly back to the reception desk. The woman's shouts and abuses continued to follow her down the long, echoing corridor: "I have a gun! I'm not afraid to use it! I know what you're here for, and you can't have it! I have a gun!" Summer approached the nurse on duty.

"Excuse me, I must have had the wrong room. I was looking for Magda."

"Magda? She should've been in there . . ."

"No, there was someone else in there. She seemed a bit distraught— said she had a gun . . ."

"Oh, well, that's Phyllis. She shouldn't be in there." The nurse rose from her desk.

"She's also wearing Magda's nightgown and slippers," Summer said.

"Well, let's go get to the bottom of this, shall we?"

The nurse marched briskly back to the room where Phyllis was meant to be, assuming that if she was in Magda's room, Magda was probably in hers. She gave a soft knock on the door, and Magda's familiar voice answered from within.

"Magda! Sweetheart, why are you in Phyllis's room?" the nurse asked, hands on her hips. Summer peered nervously in at Magda, who sat in the distinctly smaller room in a chair by a window wearing her same old clothes and shabby green beanie over the same rough silver braids.

"Nurse Mason! I'm so sorry to worry you. Nothing is wrong."

"Sweetheart, Phyllis is in your room, and your friend here says she's wearing your nighty and slippers. What's going on? Did she bully you or scare you? You know she doesn't really have a gun, Dear." Magda looked past the nurse at Summer, who was peeking timidly around the nurse's back.

"No, no, it's all perfectly straightforward. Poor Phyllis hasn't had a new nighty in a very long time, and she said hers has been scratchy and unpleasant. She also hasn't had a visit from anyone in far too long, and since her window overlooks this fringe of trees, she doesn't even get to see the people coming and going from the building. She used to enjoy watching other people's children and grandchildren come visiting from the window in her old room. I let her have my room since it has a front view, and I took her view of the trees. She's more comfortable in the nighty Summer packed for me, and I'm happier with a view of the trees—I like to see the birds. There's nothing wrong here, I promise. It was a perfectly fair trade."

"But Magda, your friend arranged especially for you to have a bigger room, and that nighty was for you! How long has it been since *you* had a new nighty?" Nurse Mason was looking Magda up and down, examining her shabby old clothes.

"I'm happy with what I have. And now Phyllis is happy, too."

"She didn't *seem* very happy." Summer finally ventured.

"She's fearful of strangers. She has dementia, Summer, so nearly everyone is a stranger to her now. You of all people should be understanding." Summer felt duly shamed. She was, after all, going to be a psychiatrist. She couldn't take things so personally. She was just confused and embarrassed to find the wrong person in Magda's room wearing the clothes she'd carefully picked out for her friend.

"Well, if Miss Summer is okay with the room change, I don't have a problem with it. I can have the sheets swapped out so that you both start off fresh. You really should ask next time, you know. We have a protocol for sanitation, and we don't just go trading rooms willy-nilly."

"I'm sorry! I was just talking with poor Phyllis in the recreation room this morning, and she was so sad! I felt like it would be an easy thing to make better without troubling you. I know how busy you are doing your good work."

"Wait, she talked to you, Magda?" Nurse Mason looked impressed. "She doesn't talk much, and when she does, she's usually making threats and yelling at 'intruders.'" Magda just smiled. "Well, it's good of you to interact with her. She doesn't get many visitors these days—and speaking of visitors!" She turned to Summer, who smiled and waved feebly at Magda. "Magda, would you like to take your guest to the recreation room to talk? I'll get an orderly to come change your sheets and clean the surfaces while you have your visit."

***

Summer and Magda sat down in two armchairs by a large window. A pair of elderly men played checkers at a table in the corner, and on the sofa, a frail great-grandmother in a pink paper mask was meeting a tiny new baby while the mother took pictures on her phone. Summer couldn't bring herself to look Magda in the eye and kept fiddling with her styrofoam cup of instant coffee and clearing her throat. Magda's smiling eyes watched her, peering over her mask just as they had peered over the fence only a week earlier.

"Magda, I'm sorry about this . . ." Summer began. She paused, hoping Magda would rescue her by filling the pause with reassurances that all was forgiven. She glanced hopefully up at Magda's eyes. "Are you angry with your girl?" she finally asked, tears choking her throat.

"Honestly, I don't know how you knew, you clever girl," Magda said cheerfully. "But maybe you *didn't* know. Maybe it was just one of those happy accidents, or maybe you were sent." Magda sighed contentedly and gazed out the window.

"What do you mean? Knew what?"

"That last thing . . . that last attachment. The thing I couldn't give up." Magda looked at Summer reassuringly. "My cave, Summer. I could never have left it on my own—that old house. Maxim's love and sweat and effort built it for us all those years ago. That garden—my little cairn . . . I know I should have left it all long ago. Taking me from it was a mercy, Summer. Severe . . ." she looked at Summer askance with one eyebrow raised. " . . . yes, severe, but a mercy none the less."

"I'm still sorry. I only meant for you to have what you need. You deny yourself all these necessities—"

"Comforts. And you denied me the one comfort I was loath to renounce—my last little connection to the past—to Maxim and to Blaise—to my lost baby. I don't think I ever could have left it if you hadn't made me. But now! Now maybe I can finally do it!"

"Do what, Magda?"

"Become human, of course!" Magda said with a wink. Summer laughed, if only because it seemed like Magda wanted her to.

"Human! What have you been up until now? A bird?"

"Oh, if only! If only. No, I've been something dreadful! But maybe now, because of you, I can finally find her!"

"Find who?"

"*Her*. The Magda I was meant to be. How frustrating it's been to be stuck like this!"

"Stuck in the house?"

"No, no. Stuck out on the bottom rung. Stuck on the threshold. Stuck with this one last thing . . . this one last attachment that I just couldn't shake. I've wanted for so long to be rid of it—wanted it and dreaded it. I had hoped to be able to do it alone. That was silly. No one can do it alone. I knew I needed help. I'd known for a while and finally asked. I didn't know what that help would look like, but I suppose it looks like you! My beautiful Summer-Sunshine!"

"I'm glad you aren't mad, but I can't say I quite understand why you aren't. I feel terrible! If you'd just had a bed! If you'd had light and heat and a full pantry and a place to sleep—I would never have dreamed . . ."

"It's a good thing I had already renounced so much, or you wouldn't have helped me!" she laughed. "It's ironic, really!"

"Magda, I just don't understand why you want to live this way! Why do you want so little? Why do you want to deny yourself every comfort—every attachment—everything, and then you're so concerned about other people having all the petty little things they want! You give people food from your garden when they already have full pantries, and it's all you have! You give your nighty away to someone who already has one—just because hers is scratchy? You . . . you're so concerned . . . so sympathetic and kind . . . to-ward everyone but yourself! I can't understand why you won't take care of yourself! It's not selfish to love yourself, take care of yourself, and make your own happiness a priority. I'm trying! I'm trying to help and to make sure you have what you need—what you deserve!"

"Deserve?" Magda looked at Summer, her eyes serious and strangely humorless. "Summer, wisdom is knowing yourself well enough to know you deserve death." Summer stared at Magda in shock.

"You deserve no such thing, Magda! You deserve life! You deserve comfort and love and cookies whenever you want them! You deserve the big room, the soft nighty, and visits every day from people who love you! From me! I love you!" Magda closed the six-foot gap between them and took Summer in a firm embrace, holding her quietly.

"Sometimes love is different than you'd think, Summer—not spoiling and pampering and cajoling. Sometimes love is letting someone have what they need, even if it isn't what you want for them."

11

Phyllis

Why must Magda be so severe upon herself? What did it all mean? What was it all for? These questions troubled Summer as she sat by her fireplace that night with a mug of tea in her hand, and Cat curled up by her side. It was intolerable, wasn't it? Intolerable. Why should Magda be permitted to sleep on the ground or the floor, to eat dandelions from her neighbors' yards, to give away most of the good things she grew in her garden? Summer had done right to ensure her proper care, hadn't she? It wasn't unreasonable to want Magda to have something so basic as regular, balanced meals, a bed, and a change of clothes. It wasn't as if she was trying to force Magda into the lap of luxury. But now it was all happening again. Magda wouldn't stop at giving away her nice room and soft nighty and slippers. She wouldn't stop until she had nothing left at all, and then she would still find something more to give.

Summer decided to speak with the nurse—Nurse Mason seemed like a humane, reasonable woman. Maybe if she could get her to understand the situation, she could keep her updated on Magda's behavior and have an ally on the inside. If Summer could just let her know Magda's tendencies toward unnecessary and extreme austerity, she could get Nurse Mason to lay down the law where she herself had failed. In the meantime, Summer would go and buy another nighty—another pair of cozy slippers—and maybe a few friendly touches for Magda's much smaller room. A wall mirror might give the illusion of spaciousness. A plant would give Magda something living to care for. She would do it tomorrow and have a talk with Nurse Mason before seeing Magda.

Nurse Mason was kind, patient, and understanding. She listened to Summer's explanations about Magda's ascetical tendencies with concern and empathy, promising to keep an eye on things and make sure Magda had what she needed. This soothed Summer's worries, and she felt a little lighter as she entered the recreation room for her visit with Magda that day.

"You get out of here!" a fragile, wavering voice shrieked as she entered the room. Phyllis was in a chair by the door as if poised and waiting for Summer's arrival. "I told you to get out!" she repeated with a weak crack in her voice.

"Hello! It's Phyllis, isn't it?" Summer said soothingly.

"Don't you dare! Don't make me get my gun! I'll use it, you know! Don't think I won't!"

"You don't need to do that. I'm just here to see Magda. You know Magda. I'm her friend." Phyllis's stony eyes softened slightly.

"Magda?" she asked.

"Yes, Magda is my dearest, best friend. I'm here to see her. I've brought her some cookies. Would you like to have one, too?" Phyllis's eyes turned hard again.

"Nurse! Nurse Mason! Come quick! This woman is trying to poison me! Where's my gun? Who's hidden my gun? You'd better get out of here! I'm getting my gun, and I'll use it! I'll blow your head off! I will! I have a gun!"

"I'm sorry I bothered you. I'm just going to go find Magda now."

"Don't you go near her! I'll shoot you!" Phyllis was shaking with rage and fear, holding her hand in a tight fist with one finger pointing out at Summer like a gun. Magda came over from the other side of the room and knelt by Phyllis's chair.

"Please don't shoot my friend, Dear," Magda said in all seriousness. She wrapped her arms around Phyllis and laid her head on the woman's thin, heaving chest. "Do you know? I can hear your heart beating in there! I can hear that good, kind, gentle heart of yours just beating away! Summer, do you know what a good heart my Phyllis has?"

"I don't doubt it," Summer said, watching in awe as Magda ran her fingers tenderly through Phyllis's unkempt hair.

"Phyllis is good. Phyllis is very much loved. Magda loves Phyllis and won't let anyone ever hurt her." A childlike smile spread across Phyllis's face as she patted Magda's head with her gnarled, arthritic hand, stroking the silver braids and kissing the top of her old green beanie. "You really should have one of Summer's cookies, Dear. They're very tasty. Trust me—I've had them before." Summer took a cookie from her plastic container and handed it to Phyllis.

"I baked them just this morning," Summer said. Phyllis eyed the cookie with suspicion. Magda quickly took one for herself, pulled down her mask, and shoved it into her mouth whole, making exaggerated noises of enjoyment. Phyllis laughed, finally tasting the cookie.

"See? I told you my friend makes good cookies. And you know, she has a dog!" Phyllis looked at Summer with sudden interest. "Yes, a beautiful dog with stripes like a tiger and one blue eye and one brown eye. And Dear, she calls it Cat! What do you think of that!" Phyllis laughed, her mouth still full of cookie crumbs. "Phyllis likes dogs. She used to have one before she came here."

"Oh, really? What was your dog's name?"

"Rabbit," she said sheepishly.

"Really? How funny! Was he very soft, like a rabbit?"

"Fast."

"And did he like carrots?"

"Who?"

"Rabbit, your dog."

"How do you know about Rabbit? Have you been talking to Bruce?"

"Who's Bruce?"

"I'll shoot you!" Phyllis pointed her finger at Summer's face again.

"She doesn't know your Bruce, Phyllis. You told her about Rabbit just now."

"Did I?"

"Yes. You were talking about dogs."

"Tell him I miss him . . ." Phyllis said to Summer as she looked down at her own slippered feet. "Tell him, won't you . . . when you see him? Tell him I miss him. Why doesn't he come to see me anymore?"

"She doesn't know him, Dear. But why don't we all go and sit by the window and see what else Summer has brought with her today." The three of them sat in chairs by the window, and Summer produced a red gift bag. She handed it to Magda, who peered inside. "Oh, Phyllis! Would you look at this! How did she know! How do you think my friend knew you needed another nighty!" Magda pulled the new nightgown from the bag and laid it across Phyllis's lap. "Feel it! It's so soft!"

"But, Magda—"

"Phyllis had a little accident with the other, and it had to go away, and Phyllis has been so sad to be without it! Thank you, Summer! Isn't my friend nice, Phyllis? I told you she was a good one!" Phyllis's eyes misted over as she rubbed the new nightgown on her wrinkled cheek.

"Well, Magda . . ." Summer faltered, "I had gotten it for—"

"So thoughtful! So kind is my girl, Summer. Let's see what else she's put in here. Well now, my goodness! Would you look at this!" Phyllis gasped and clutched at Magda's arm. "Weren't we just talking about how much you used to like working in your garden? And now she's brought you a plant of your very own to keep in your room!"

"It's a golden pothos," Phyllis said. "I know it. It likes the indoors."

"It certainly does. You are so kind, Summer. We were just talking about these things, and here you are bringing them to us! What a treat! What a kindness!"

"Well, my intention was—"

"You have beautiful intentions, Summer. And now my two beautiful friends can be friends with each other! Isn't that right, Phyllis? You can be friends with Summer now too, and she'll come and visit us both!" Phyllis could barely take her eyes off the plant and the new nightgown on her lap. A tear rolled down her creased cheek. Magda squeezed her hand.

Summer played along for the remainder of their visit. She had hoped to talk with Magda about her life at the nursing home and encourage her to listen to Nurse Mason and be more gentle with herself. Still, the entire conversation centered around Magda telling Phyllis about Summer, her beautiful dog, Cat—which made Phyllis laugh every time—about the garden she used to keep, and all the delicious produce Summer was going to harvest from it and bring to them when it was ripe. When it was time to leave, Magda hugged Summer, then Phyllis came over to her and hugged her as well.

"Thank you for visiting me, Cat," Phyllis said.

"Summer."

"No, no. Autumn is here now. I've been watching the leaves fall from my window."

12

The Prodigal Son

And autumn really had truly arrived. That late October brought darker, cooler mornings and a spicy smell on the breeze. The maple tree at the park where Summer took Cat walking glowed red like the embers in her fireplace. The daylight had a different slant, a distant, older feeling. Summer was back on campus with new safety protocols to avoid the spread of illness. Life seemed to be moving along again, even with Magda missing from the house next door. When Summer couldn't manage a visit, she called Nurse Mason for updates.

"How is Magda doing? Is she being cooperative and settling in?"

"Everyone loves Magda. She's such a kookie little sweetheart! Always looking to help out her neighbors and even the staff." Summer sighed in relief. Yes, that sounded like Magda.

"So, no cause for concern, then?"

"Well, I'm not sure. She seems happy enough, but I have my eye on some things. You know, she still doesn't sleep in her bed."

"What? Doesn't sleep in her bed?"

"No, but many of our residents sleep in their chairs—it's just easier for them that way—easier to get back up, you know. But I'm not convinced that's what she's doing. It's hard to say since no one has ever seen her sleeping. Not once."

"What, never?"

"Nope. Any time one of us looks in on her, even at night, she's awake and on her feet and doing things."

"Doing what, specifically?"

"Singing mostly, I guess."

"Oh, that. That's no surprise. She sings a lot, always the same song."

"Yes, that's right. She's always singing it, humming it. It's not disruptive or loud. It doesn't bother anyone—it's just always there. But I'm not sure when she's sleeping, and that's what concerns me. I mean, she must, but just at odd times. It would probably be good for her to get onto a regular schedule. Maybe you can speak with her about it."

"I'll bring it up. I'd like to visit with Magda in her room today, if possible, rather than the recreation room. I might have a better chance of actually having that discussion if we're alone."

"Sure, I'll see to it that she's in her room during visiting hours today if you'd like to come by and see her."

When Summer entered Magda's little room, she was singing softly and taping plastic sandwich bags to her window in neat rows. There were eight of them taped along the window with what appeared to be a paper towel in each.

"Hi, Magda! What are you up to today?" Magda's eye's crinkled in a mischievous smile.

"I have a new friend—in the kitchen."

"Oh? And what have they given you?"

"Jessica."

"What did Jessica give you?"

"Bags!"

"I can see that—what are you doing with them?"

"I'm sprouting beans! Look! She let me take some dry pinto beans. I have them wrapped in wet paper towel, and the baggies are like little greenhouses for them! See? I get some nice morning sunshine on this window."

"Well, aren't you clever! Take you out of your garden, and you'll still find a way to grow one, wherever you are!"

"How *is* the garden? Are you visiting it? The weeds will be taking over by now."

"Don't worry about that. I go over to your garden every evening and take care of the weeds."

"And the green beetles?"

"What about them?"

"Look, I need you to collect them. Don't kill them—just collect them."

"What ever for, Magda?"

"They're invasive and very damaging to the garden."

"Why not just get a pesticide?"

"No, no. That's no good for the birds that eat them. But look, the kudzu is invasive too, so this is what you do: You take the beetles away from the garden and put them on the kudzu."

"That's a lot of trouble, Magda . . . that's what you've been doing with the beetles in your little pillbox all this time?"

"It's the best option, I promise. I get the green beetles out of my garden without killing them or harming the birds, and they help keep the kudzu from taking over. They're both aggressive invaders, you see. They deserve each other."

"Okay . . . well, I'll see what I can do . . ."

"Now, the zucchinis—they're probably enormous by now."

"They're big, yes. I'll bring some to you soon."

"Well, listen—this is important. I give some to all the neighbors. I need you to put a sack-full on each doorstep. I'll make you a list of instructions before you leave if you need help remembering what to do. What's left after you've taken the neighbors theirs, you split between yourself and Jessica. I told her you'd be bringing them when they're ready, so she's expecting them. She said she would make us ratatouille!"

"I'll do my best. It's a lot of zucchini—like I said, some of them are huge!" Summer sat down cross-legged on the end of Magda's bed. "This is a very comfortable bed!" Summer said, patting it admiringly and steering the conversation to her own purpose. "I bet you sleep well here." Magda just smiled and continued fiddling with her window bags.

"Are *you* sleeping well, Summer? No more nightmares or anxious sleep disturbances, I hope."

"Oh, I'm fine, but what about you? I know it's a big change coming to stay here after so long in the same place. It would be understandable if it's taking time to get used to the change. How has your sleep been?"

"I get what I need."

"Is the bed comfortable?"

"I'm sure it is, as you say."

"Oh, have you been sleeping in the chair, then?"

"No. No, I don't sleep in the chair. It's comfortable to sit on, though. I like to sit and watch the birds in the trees most mornings. Sometimes silly squirrels chase each other up and down the trunks. I saw one recently that only had half a tail. Maybe a coyote got the other half . . . do you think you could bring me some sunflower seeds to set outside the window? For the cardinals? Even when I can't see them, I hear their chip-chip.' Maybe they'd come for a visit."

"Yes, if it's all right with Nurse Mason—but Magda, where do you sleep?"

"You worry too much, sweet girl. Do I look ill? Do I look like I'm suffering from any deprivations of sleep or food or anything else?"

"No, I suppose you look the same as you always have."

"That's right. I'm fine. Now Phyllis, on the other hand—I *am* worried about her."

"Why? What's going on?"

"Her Bruce came yesterday."

"Who is Bruce?"

"He's her son. He's very busy—too busy to visit very often, and I've never actually seen him."

"Well, it's good he came, then, isn't it?"

"Maybe." Magda knit her brow.

"Why? What happened?"

"He met with her in her room, like this, but do you know what he did?"

"What?"

"She told me that he took off his mask."

"He didn't!"

"She told me that he said he couldn't breathe with it on and took it right off and left it off the full thirty minutes he was here. He said he thought it would be okay since they were in her room and not the rec room with everyone else."

"He shouldn't have done that—here of all places. He could have exposed her! How irresponsible!"

"I'm concerned for her. You've seen her, Summer. She's frail."

"Maybe it'll be okay. Maybe he was healthy."

"Maybe . . ." They sat in silence for a moment. Summer's scalp began to tingle as she felt her blood begin to boil.

"Oh, that just burns me up! You know? Why aren't people thinking of others? Some people wear masks all day, every day for their work—look at Nurse Mason! Why is it so hard to wear one for a short visit or a shopping trip? They should educate themselves and think about other people! I could just . . . just . . ."

"Just what?"

"I could hit him! I could really . . . just . . . hit him!"

"You're angry, Summer."

"Well, yeah! Aren't you? There is such a thing as righteous anger when someone has been absolutely stupid and selfish!"

"There is such a thing, but I wouldn't assume that's what you're experiencing. You weren't even there. You don't know him. You barely know Phyllis. You're enjoying it too much."

"Enjoying it? I'm furious!"

"Fury is enjoyable."

"I'm absolutely not enjoying it!" Summer's eyes blazed with indignation, her fists clenched in her lap. Magda just laughed.

"Of course you are, Summer. Everyone enjoys a nice, hot rage. It makes us feel strong. Potent. Powerful."

"I feel helpless!"

"Oh, I doubt that. You're thinking about all things you would do to that poor man in his weakness. Not everyone is so strong—so resolute. Or so healthy."

"It doesn't take extraordinary resolve or strength to wear a mask in a nursing home! Oh, I'd like to kick him senseless! Or at least write him a very loud letter!" Magda laughed again.

"You really are indulging in it now. I bet you can see the whole scene in your mind! You can see him on the floor. You're probably picturing him very ugly, too, aren't you?"

"Of course he's ugly! That's an ugly thing to do!"

"I suppose you've given him a double chin and green Covid boogers!" Summer stared at Magda speechless, then burst out laughing. They both laughed unrestrainedly until they were struggling to catch their breath and were wiping away tears.

"But why aren't you mad, Magda? Phyllis is your friend."

"I'm concerned, but anger at him is only love of myself and my own sense of what's right."

"Self-love is healthy, Magda. I've told you time and time again—you have to love yourself! If you don't love yourself, how can you expect anyone else to? Self-love is the starting point—the goal of a healthy, well-adjusted life!" Magda laid her hand on Summer's and squeezed it firmly.

"My dear Summer, you are young. You are so very young, and you have just found a thing that you really mean. You've heard it so much that it must be true. It may only be partly true—slightly true—but you say it again and again with such force and heat, simply because you are so very young, and you've finally found something to mean. Well, brace yourself, Summer. I'm going to tell you something that you must really hear and try very hard to remember: Self-love is only a friend to itself—a Self that's not even real. It is the lover of an illusion and the hater of all."

"So what? We should hate ourselves? Beat ourselves up and punish ourselves? Starve ourselves? Deprive ourselves of every comfort?"

"No, Summer. Not hate ourselves. We should *know* ourselves and be humbled." Summer didn't know what to say. She simply stared at Magda. "Now, don't look at me like that, Summer. Your face has never been inscrutable to me. I see those worried thoughts carved between your brows as usual. I know you don't think it's healthy. You wish I would wash the sand out of my mind—take a lavender-scented bath—eat the chocolate and the cheese—the eggs and the flesh meats. You want me to care for myself—love myself—take time for myself—buy something pretty for myself—sleep through the night in a soft bed."

"Self-care is the first step toward self-love," Summer recited, "and self-love is the goal. Just be reasonable."

"I left reason on a distant shore when I set out across this expanse of scorching sand in search of the old, deep wells. You want me to live for my own sake. What you don't yet realize is that I stayed here in the desert for my own sake. This life, this way of living it, is, in a sense for me, because I care for myself enough to deny the comforts that keep me weak. Would you be happier if my gymnasium had assorted weights and treadmills?"

"It's not healthy, Magda—for your body or your mind."

"Well, thank you, truly. Thank you for caring enough to tell me that I have lost my mind."

"I didn't say that."

"But you're thinking it. At this point its loss doesn't concern me since it's my soul that I've been digging through these hot desert sands to find. I may have left my cave, but I'm still in the desert, and here I will stay."

13

Bad News

Morning broke like an egg fallen from a nest on a windy night. Orange rays oozed over the misty autumn treetops as Summer walked Cat around the neighborhood. The day would warm up quickly, as days will do when the sun is unimpeded by cloud. Cat was straining at her leash to chase a squirrel that mocked her from a mossy tree trunk when Summer's phone summoned her with a buzz.

"Ma'am, this is Nurse Mason. I'm calling to let you know that our nursing facility is in full lockdown now. We have a confirmed Covid-19 case and will not be allowing visitors until further notice. We're setting up online chats for family and friends to communicate with our residents by appointment, and as always, you can call your friend on the landline in her room."

"I'm so sorry to hear this . . . can you tell me who's ill? Is it serious?"

"We're keeping the patient's identity confidential as per HIPPA and our own privacy regulations, but I can confirm that it is serious. All of our residents are considered vulnerable, but rest assured that we are doing our best to be vigilant and to keep everyone safe amid this crisis. We do recommend that you be tested yourself since you were here recently."

"Okay. Yes, I will. Thank you for letting me know."

It was Phyllis. It had to be. That irresponsible son of hers had made her sick, and now everyone was in danger. Magda was in danger. Magda, who couldn't keep her distance—wouldn't keep her distance. Magda, who probably hugged Phyllis every day and breathed the very air from her lungs in the process. Summer's heart ached with the fear of losing her friend.

In the past year, something had changed in their relationship. Magda had gone from being a problem to solve, a project, an experiment, a case study, to being an absolute necessity. Indeed, Summer felt her need for Magda so profoundly and secretly that she only realized the intensity of that need when faced with the fear of losing her forever. How or when this need had come to be, Summer could hardly say. But Magda, in her own strange way, had been caring for Summer and understanding her on a level she hadn't believed possible. She couldn't lose her now.

Surely—surely Magda needed her just as much—the woman who had spent so many years alone, grieving over her past and punishing herself for things that weren't her fault. Now she couldn't even see Magda in person. Couldn't love her and tell her to be kind to herself. Couldn't make sure she was eating well, sleeping well, thinking well. Couldn't take her cookies and zucchinis and nightgowns she wouldn't wear. It was a disaster.

It worried Summer. It upset her digestion, constricted her chest, and disturbed her sleep. What if Magda had been exposed? What if Magda were to become ill? What if Magda died? She imagined herself knocking on Bruce's door and screaming in his face . . . screaming, shouting in his dumb, ugly, flabby face. Then, she would pull a baseball bat from behind her back and hit him. She would hit him and hit him and hit him. Of course she knew she shouldn't hit him. Of course she knew she shouldn't think such things, but it was this recurrent thought that kept coming to her that night after learning of the Covid case in the nursing home: Phyllis's illness. It bothered her and filled her with guilt, but she couldn't quite let go of it. It would be a solution, wouldn't it? To the ache of loss? Like bashing in the smiling face of a naked porcelain doll. But no! Nothing was lost yet! She was burying Magda and beating up Bruce in anticipation of something that might never happen.

Summer was low the next day, drinking coffee and staring from her window when Nurse Mason called. Magda wanted to speak with her.

"Hello? Magda?"

"Summer . . . stop it."

"What? What do you mean?"

"You know what I mean. Stop it."

"Are you feeling okay? Are you staying in your room? Washing your hands? Wearing your mask?"

"I'm fine. It's you I'm worried about."

"Well, don't. Worry about Phyllis. I'm assuming it's her who's got it? How is she—do you know? Have you heard anything?"

"She's struggling. She has weak lungs anyway."

"Oh no . . ."

"She doesn't know what's going on. Or if she does, she's hiding it well. She does tend to ignore unpleasant things and expect them to go away on their own. Death doesn't run away into woods, no matter how much you pretend you don't see it . . . or chase it with an imaginary gun."

"Magda, are you saying you've actually seen her? You've actually been in that room with her? Please, please tell me you haven't gone anywhere near her."

"I'm fine, Summer. But you—"

"Look! I don't know what you think you know, but you don't! I'm fine!" Summer was becoming defensive now. She didn't mean to snap at Magda, but in her stress and worry, she did.

"Well . . . you stay safe, Dear," Magda said at last. "Hug Cat for me—and tend the garden. You won't forget?"

"I won't. Don't worry."

Summer ended the call feeling unsettled and exposed. What could Magda possibly know about her own private fears and dreams? Maybe she had meant something else. Maybe if she'd let Magda say what she meant . . . but the fear. She didn't want to know what Magda knew. She didn't want to hear it spoken aloud. Summer stroked Cat's back furiously until the dog went to lie down elsewhere. How could Magda know these things?

Three days passed—agonizing, stifling, and maddeningly long days. Summer heard nothing from Magda. She feared calling her and being scolded for heaven knows what. She didn't deserve it. She'd been like a granddaughter to Magda, and she didn't deserve to be shamed, especially for things Magda knew nothing about—things she couldn't possibly know about. Eventually, Summer settled on calling Nurse Mason for an update on the state of things at the nursing home.

"Well, I'm not really supposed to talk about other patients, but since Magda is so close with her . . . pretty much the only person here who is . . . it's my opinion that the end is near. I don't expect that Phyllis will live through the night." Summer could barely respond. It had all happened so fast!

"And . . . still no other cases? Magda?"

"She's perfectly healthy. No symptoms. Nothing out of the ordinary. Everyone else has been fine as well. It's just poor Phyllis at this point."

"I'm . . . yeah . . . I'm just really sorry to hear that this has happened. Does Bruce know?"

"Oh, you knew Bruce?"

"Well, not exactly."

"He died, Summer. Three nights ago. He'd been ill as well. He was severely asthmatic, you know. Had a tough time wearing a mask but couldn't stay home from his job. He was considered an 'essential worker.' Poor man . . . at least they were able to see each other one last time."

"I . . . I'm sorry, Nurse Mason. I've got to go!"

Summer ran to the toilet and threw up. Guilt wracked her mind even as sickness wracked her body. She lay on her bed with her face buried deep in a pillow and screamed into its muffled softness for the first time since she was a little girl. Cat jumped on top of her and nipped at her ear, growling playfully. When Summer didn't move to embrace her and wrestle, the dog groaned and curled up next to her mistress, who didn't move from that spot for the remainder of the day but drifted into a fitful sleep.

14

The Call

Summer was brushing her teeth when the call came. It was the kind of day when one expects to receive unsettling news. The sky was filled with ragged clouds of an unnatural, smoldering pink, and the wind sent chaotic hordes of fallen leaves scraping and tumbling down the road into heaps along the gutters and fence lines. The fireplace smoke streamed horizontally from the chimney like the stack from an old steam train hurtling down the tracks toward certain disaster. It was the kind of day when anything could happen.

When Summer answered the call, it was the same patient voice that always greeted her when she made inquiries about Magda. Perhaps it was an update on Phyllis. If Nurse Mason had been correct, she had probably passed away that night, and that, of course, would be sad, but not unexpected. Perhaps they would be allowing visitors again soon, after an appropriate length of quarantine to make sure no other cases arose. She found herself thinking that a walk with Magda on a little less windy day than this would be lovely—under the red, orange, and yellow canopy of leaves. Magda would be sad for a while, of course. She had been fond of Phyllis, but Summer would take her cookies, maybe a pumpkin loaf with toasted pecans. They would walk arm-in-arm around the grounds as they had before, and Summer would cheer her up with stories about Cat's antics and the birds in the garden. She would bring one of the pumpkins from Magda's patch. Maybe Jessica would cook it up and put it in a pie or something for her. However, the voice that greeted her on the phone had a tremulous quality—a hesitation that made Summer feel uneasy.

"Has Phyllis passed? So sad. I'm sure her loss will be felt by all who knew her . . . will you be opening up to visitors soon?

"Well, no, Summer—we won't be taking visitors for some time yet."

"I thought hers was the only case. Is she still . . . is she still with us?"

"She's better. Phyllis is much, much better this morning."

"Wow! Really? Well . . . that's wonderful!"

"I know. We didn't expect her to pull through. It defies everything we thought we knew about this virus, but last night her fever broke, her coughing eased up, her breathing cleared, and she was out of bed this morning, yelling at the orderly, looking for her gun. We're all scratching our heads. It's really something."

"Well, that's good news! Magda will be glad she's better. I know they were friendly before all of this."

"Yes, ma'am. . ." There was that hesitation again. What wasn't she saying?

"Is everything all right? With Magda, I mean?"

"No . . . no it's not. We're worried. Magda got sick last night—very suddenly—very unexpectedly. She was fine—her old self—then, *boom!*"

"What is it? What's wrong with her? Did she eat something bad?"

"No, nothing like that. It's unusual compared with other cases. There's usually more of a warning . . . a lead-up. A sort of steady decline from the onset of the initial symptoms . . . you would think she was in the final stages . . . picking up where Phyllis left off."

"Oh no . . . Covid?"

"That's what it looks like. Magda has a very high fever and has terrible trouble breathing, but it just happened so quickly, like I said. We have her on a respirator now . . . we won't have test results back for a while yet to even confirm that's what it is. In the meantime, it's not looking good. We're doing what we can, but—"

"But what?"

" . . . well . . ."

"Is she dying?"

"I'm just saying, Miss Magda asked for an attorney and a priest."

"She did? When?"

"Yesterday. It's strange, really. We found her in the hall. She's been good about staying in her room, but last night she was out. We saw her outside of Phyllis's door. Maybe she wanted to say goodbye, but we told her it wasn't safe."

"My God. What was she thinking . . ."

"It was then that she asked for a priest and an attorney. We thought she meant for Phyllis. We told her Phyllis's affairs were already in order, but she said it was for her. She asked for them before she was taken ill. Before she had any symptoms at all. Maybe she felt it coming."

"It wouldn't be that surprising. She always seems to see things coming. And me? Did she ask for me?"

"No, ma'am. We couldn't let you in anyway."

"But did she ask to call me? To talk?"

"No, ma'am. But even that's not possible now. She's not able to speak. She didn't actually ask for you to be notified at all, but I thought you'd want to know what's going on. I know you're close—there's no one else to notify, and I'm sure she just didn't want to upset you. You know how she is."

"Upset me? I . . . yes . . . yes, thank you for calling and letting me know. I really appreciate it. Please keep me posted."

Summer ended the call and took a few slow breaths, trying to slow her heart rate. An attorney and a priest—but Magda hadn't asked for her? Even to talk with her on the phone? They were practically family. Why wouldn't she have called Summer or at least asked that she be notified, rather than the nurse having to decide to make the call on her own? Summer wandered around the house—opening the refrigerator—closing the refrigerator— looking out the window, then she decided:

"Forget this! I'm going!"

Summer slipped on her shoes and leapt into her car. Her foot was heavy, and she kept catching herself speeding. She rounded the corner and saw the nursing home approach, but it was too late. She knew when she saw the flashing lights in her rearview mirror that they were coming for Magda. She veered onto the shoulder to let them pass, and sure enough, the ambulance pulled up to the front door. As she pulled in and parked, she saw Nurse Mason talking to the paramedics. Why weren't they going in? Why were they just talking? She watched as they took the stretcher out of the ambulance, slowly.

"Hurry!" Summer said aloud as her car idled in its spot. "Stop wasting time!"

She didn't dare approach, knowing she would be turned away. She waited and watched, barely breathing. Then it came—the stretcher, the fig- ure covered from head to toe, the priest with his long gray beard poking out from the bottom of his black face mask. Magda. She knew it was Magda. Summer leapt from the car and ran to the front door forgetting her mask.

"Ma'am! Keep back!"

"I'm her friend!"

"You need to keep your distance!" the paramedic ordered, a purple gloved hand held up like a traffic guard.

"But we're. . . family!"

"Keep back!"

"Are you Summer, but any chance?" the priest asked.

"Yes—yes, I'm Summer."

"Magda left this for you. I took the dictation myself, so she never touched it. It's safe." He extended a gloved hand, holding a folded piece of paper. "May her memory be eternal."

Summer sat in her car, unable to move. She should have had more time! How could this have happened so quickly? She was well just yesterday. That's not how this virus works! She couldn't be healthy one day and dead the next! It wasn't fair! And Phyllis! How could she! How could she live? How could she be healthy, and Magda die? Summer could barely breathe. This couldn't be real. It must be a dream—a terrible, terrible dream. She glanced down at the folded piece of paper. She picked it up, her hand trembling and weak, and slowly, silently read the words inside.

"Oh Magda . . . what have you done?"

15

Into the Desert

Perhaps it would have ended this way anyway, even without a kookie old lady with missing teeth, a beautiful garden, and strange desert stories, but it's unlikely. Summer would have become a child psychiatrist because once she started something, she finished it—and finished it better than anyone else could have. Perhaps it was because she had something to prove, or perhaps it was because of everything she had lost, but she never gave anything less than her all.

Maybe Summer would have changed directions anyway—taken an interest in monasticism, made peace with her parents, and taken up regular tree climbing, but it's not likely. How different that year might have looked, had she not been forced to stay home—had she not listened to Magda's stories most evenings, eaten her pickles and peaches, climbed her pecan tree, and dreamed painful dreams.

Summer sat on her red sofa, not by a fireplace with pine-scented candles, but by a window—the window that overlooked the garden—the garden she'd kept impeccably weeded over the past three years. The garden where an oddly shaped dog with one blue eye and one brown eye roamed freely, unhindered from eating worms and chasing fireflies, treeing squirrels, and barking at the garden hose. The garden where she grew the giant zucchinis that magically appeared on all the neighbors' doorsteps each year. The garden with the green beetles that she never killed but always dutifully transferred to the kudzu as she'd been taught. The garden with the bench under the apple tree where she sat every evening singing a strange song, as well as she could remember it—a song that flowed in and out of itself, shimmering, shaking, colorful like a soap bubble.

Summer had lived there alone with Cat, in the house that Maxim built—the cave that Magda left her—while visiting the nursing home daily to sit with a lonely old woman who threatened to shoot her every time she came, bearing freshly baked cookies and pickles from her garden. The pickles were never quite as good as Magda's, but they weren't at all bad.

Summer never needed Phyllis the way she had needed Magda, and Phyllis never needed her, at least not desperately. Phyllis never told her anything deep or mysterious or helpful or profound, but one thing they both took away from their visits was love. They loved each other in their own strange ways—Summer by having the same rambling conversation with her every day, soothing her worries, holding her hand, and making sure she always had a comfortable nighty. In turn, Phyllis loved Summer by never actually shooting her, finally holstering her trigger finger, and laughing a little at the stories she told about a dog named Cat and birds she had known in the desert where she had lived as a child. What more can be said? They would have been fine on their own, but they were better together. Summer was not alone while she lived in the cave, and Phyllis was not alone when she died in the nursing home.

After the funeral, still dressed in black, Summer sat on her red sofa, running her fingers over the ragged chew marks from Cat's tumultuous puppyhood. She looked out at the garden, now thick with foliage and heavy with fruit. It was almost time to go, and Summer finally said her farewells to that strange but necessary chapter of her life.

It wasn't just because she had finally finished her degree and people called her Doctor that she was leaving, but because of Magda, the garden, and because of Phyllis. She wanted to be a desert dweller on purpose now. If she had to be in the desert, she wanted to know it and feel it every moment and learn to love it. She wanted to hear the stars, smell the rain, find the deep wells, and learn to look at the Sun. Her bag was packed. The house that Maxim built was sold, all Summer's furnishings conveyed with it.

Summer sat holding a faded green clothbound book in her hand—the one item she'd found in the otherwise empty house when she took possession. It was Magda's book—her desert novel—the fictionalized, poeticized story of her exile, up to the time when she was forced to leave her cave. Summer sat with that book and with Magda's final letter to her on her lap, creased and worn from the many times she had read it, smeared with her tears. She would read it again, just one more time, and then she would leave for good:

Dearest Summer,

Don't be angry with your old Magda. I know you wanted to keep me around longer, but it's better this way. I've talked with an attorney. He'll contact you soon to let you know. I'm leaving you the cave and the garden, Dear. I hope you can find peace there for as long as it's right—and only as long as it's right. I'm also leaving you Phyllis. Visit with her often—love her well. I think you'll find that you learn something from her that I couldn't have taught you.

I know you have wanted to know the end of my exile story for a while now. I could never tell you because I didn't know it yet myself. But I believe it ends something like this:

And as she walked, the nighthawks swooped above her head, the long-absent quail trailed a little behind her, a shadowy young bobcat bounded to her right, and a large pack of coyotes trotted peacefully a little way to her left. She didn't question the plausibility of her traveling companions or her own sanity. Their presence with her seemed natural and appropriate. And as they continued on toward the east, she began to hear once again that silent singing of the stars that had gladdened her heart on that first night in the desert so many years ago. The song she had longed to hear again and which she had feared was lost forever:

. . . behold the bridegroom cometh in the middle of the night and we come and we come and we come to receive the light from the light that shines and shines the light from the light that shines always shines that is never overtaken by night so the light in the night and the bridegroom cometh and cometh and always cometh in the middle of the night and blessed is the servant whom He shall find watching always watching in the gloaming and the dawning and the shining of the gladsome light in the darksome night and the wholesome shining of the light the light that gladsome light that is never overtaken by night that light that shines now now Now that we have come to the setting of the sun which burns like fire that burns through a thicket like a flame that sets the mountains on fire, the sun the Sun that shines and shines on the world is the light of wisdom the light gladsome light of wisdom for by it those who worshipped the stars were taught by a star to adore Thee the Sun of righteousness oh gladsome light that light in the night that shines and shines and

*behold the light of evening oh Gladsome light which burns like fire
for we are consumed embraced enfolded in the fire that is Love and
light the light that shines and shines the light from the light oh shines
always shines that is never overtaken by night darksome night the
light in the night and the bridegroom cometh and always cometh in
the middle to the night now and here and now and always and ever
unto ages of ages coming and come and coming and come always
and ever and Now in the night in the middle of the night and blessed
is the servant whom He shall find watching always watching in the
shining and the gloaming and the dawning and the shining and
the light in the night and the shining of that gladsome light that is
never overtaken by night but which burns through a thicket and sets
the mountains on fire and behold the light of evening that is never
overtaken but shines and shines for he's coming he's here he's coming
to the valley of weeping and they shall walk in the light of His face
which flames like fire on the mountain it shines and it shines from
the mountain as much as they can bear it the light in the night on
the mountain holy mountain holy fountain the fountain of light and
the dove descending and Him ascending and transcending and all
that is ending is starting and ending and starting and ending and
always Now in the light from the light as he comes always comes in
the middle of the night and blessed is the servant whom He shall find
watching always watching in the shining and the gladsome light in
the night and the dove which descends with the Voice that upends
and the Word that descends and descends and ascends and ascends
in the light from the light and behold the bridegroom cometh in the
middle of the night in the middle of the night till the shouting till the
ringing till the singing and the calling for all to rejoice both those
who fasted and those who didn't for the table is ready and laden
full-laden heavy-laden yes feast ye all sumptuously in the shouting
and the ringing and the singing and the calling for the calf is fatted
so let no one go hungry no let no one be sent away hungry from the
fair and the radiant triumphal feast the feast the Feast of Feasts of
Feasts of Feasts. . .*

*Tears filled her eyes—glorious tears—for the beauty of the song, for
the beauty of the dance, for the beauty of the desert, and the journey
and her strange companions—of old wells and old stones and voices
and rain—and for the beauty of the two familiar shapes she saw in
the distance silhouetted against the growing blue dawn: A man and
a boy looking up at the stars.*

www.ingramcontent.com/pod-product-compliance
Lightning Source LLC
Chambersburg PA
CBHW051831020726
47502CB00005B/1737